LITERALLY OFFED

A PEPPER BROOKS COZY MYSTERY

ERYN SCOTT

KRISTOPHERSON PRESS

For the real-life Hamburger.
Rest in peace, Hammy.

Your wonderful, stylish soul will be greatly missed.

1

I sighed as I sank back into my camping chair and kicked my feet up onto the log next to me. Cracking open the book in my lap, I let my gaze settle onto the welcoming cream-colored pages, my attention wrapping around each wonderful word.

Birds twittered songs of sun and fresh mountain air from the surrounding trees as a gentle rush of wind flowed through the branches of the tall pines which creaked and swayed. The almost-spicy, earthy smell of a pine needle-covered forest floor, dotted with moss and mushrooms, swirled around me, kicked up by the wind.

In the echoing silence, a loud holler made me jump. I almost dropped my book when the sound was followed by a deep, bellowed, "Keg stand!"

Heartbeat pounding in my ears from the surprise, I craned my neck to watch the guys in the campsite next to me lift a burley young man with curly brown hair onto a silver keg and chant for him to, "Chug, chug, chug!"

A group of what looked to be a dozen, testosterone-filled troglodytes were taking up the two campsites to my right.

Pulling in a deep breath, I rolled my eyes. *College kids, ugh.*

Sure, I was only twenty-three and had graduated a mere year ago with my bachelor's in English—not to mention I was technically still in college, in the midst of my first year of master's course work—but these guys felt like an altogether different species. The only similarity between us appeared to be my alma mater, based on the NWU logo stamped on a few of their T-shirts.

When I'd requested to move to a different camping spot upon our arrival a few hours before—which just happened to be in the middle of a wrestling match between two of the larger brutes—the local ranger told me the park was full up. Alas, it looked as though we were stuck with them for the foreseeable future.

Turning back to my book, I slipped in my earbuds. Tom Petty and the Heartbreaker's album, *Into the Great Wide Open* drowned out the noise from the next campsite. I sighed. Petty had been one of my dad's favorites, and he'd played the music incessantly on our family camping and road trips during my childhood. I'd never appreciated Petty's twangy charm as much as I did now Dad was gone. He'd passed away just about three years ago from a heart attack, and I missed him every single day.

As Tom and the band settled into the chorus of "Learning to Fly," I returned to the pages of *Walden* by Henry David Thoreau. I smiled as I read a particularly imperious line describing how Thoreau was certain he'd never learned a single thing from an older person. While I didn't agree with the author's sentiment, I could picture my boyfriend, Alex, reading that line and using it as further proof of what a hack the man was.

We were reading *Walden* together—it had been one of

my dad's favorites, alongside *Civil Disobedience*—and from the narrowed looks and mumbling I'd observed from my boyfriend so far, it was safe to say Alex was not enjoying the transcendentalist's most famous work. Not that it was a huge surprise. My focused, practical, altruistic boyfriend didn't have a self-serving bone in his body. In addition to being a sort of old soul, Alex also had an intense respect for the older generations, especially his father, a detective in our small college town of Pine Crest.

It was going to be hard for him to look past Thoreau's wording to see the same inspiring message about simplistic living that I saw, that my dad had seen. Which was all well and good. We'd disagreed on books before. But I loved him for continuing to read and discuss with me, even when he wasn't thrilled about my selection.

I was only partway into the next Petty song when my friends returned from their trip to the restrooms down the road. Plucking out my earbuds, I paused my music as Liv and Carson walked up.

"We're gone for two minutes and Pepper's already reading," Carson said. He tsked.

Liv shook her head, not surprised. She and I had been roommates for five years now. The girl knew curling up with a good book was my go-to activity, no matter where I was.

Raising one eyebrow, Carson glanced over at our rowdy neighbors. The curly-haired man who'd been upside down minutes before was now stumbling blearily through their camp, like a drunken bowling ball knocking over folding-chair pins. He caught my gaze and winked sloppily in my direction, before collapsing onto their picnic table.

"Maybe we should head over there. Looks like a party." Carson chuckled.

Liv and I snorted in unison.

3

"I'd rather chew the bark off all these trees," Liv said flatly. "The rangers couldn't move us, then?"

I sighed. "Nope. The campground is full up because of Labor Day. They said some people only stay one night, so we might be able to move tomorrow, but until then, we're stuck with the keg-stand crew."

"Let's cross our fingers we get a new spot before Maggie, Josh, and the kids come out tomorrow night." Liv eyed the group, now setting up a ping pong table.

I seconded the sentiment. No way did I want my five-year-old niece and two-year-old nephew to witness college culture at its least refined until, well… until they *went* to college, if I could help it.

"Where's Valdez?" Carson asked, glancing around our two-tent campsite for Alex.

Suppressing a smile, I said, "Went to buy firewood at the ranger's station." He'd been so cute, rolling up his sleeves and putting on some work gloves to go out searching for wood before I'd had a chance to tell him they sold bundles.

Carson's face fell a bit.

"Don't worry. He'll be back." Liv patted Carson's chest and chuckled.

Alex and Carson had grown pretty close over the past year. And while they were very different—Carson was goofy and the life of most parties while Alex was more subdued and contemplative—they'd become the brother each had never had.

Just then the crunching of tires on the pine cone-spotted gravel sounded behind us. I was about to put on my most narrow expression and yell at our neighbors for parking in one of our spots, when I recognized the old yellow Volvo being thrown into park.

Liv sucked in a quick breath. "Oh no."

I looked back at her, shoving the words, "Liv, what did you do?" through clenched teeth.

Nate Newton—or as many of my sister's friends called him, Naked Newt—unfolded his lanky body from the old car. Nate owned the local café Liv and I frequented, Bittersweet.

My best friend pretended to smile and wave, but said, "I forgot I'd mentioned the trip to him," keeping her mouth frozen so he wouldn't see us talking.

Carson sighed. "Babe, when are you going to learn the man takes everything you say seriously? Probably remembers it word for word or writes it down in some creepy journal after you leave the coffee shop." Carson turned his hello nod into a shake of his head as he faced his girlfriend. "I'm gonna go help Alex with that firewood."

Just as Carson turned to leave, someone else climbed out of the Volvo, surprising us even more than the car's arrival had.

"Victoria?" I said aloud in my shock, recognizing one of Nate's baristas.

The meek young woman peeked out from behind her curtain of dark hair and flashed the briefest of smiles at me. Was it a smile? It could've just as easily been a painful grimace. Had Nate kidnapped her and brought her here against her will?

I walked forward, looking for any signs of bonds or a struggle. Her hands were free, however, and she clutched her elbows as she wrapped her arms around her stomach, hunching forward in her normal posture.

Seeing Victoria was unharmed, I turned to Nate. "How'd you guys…? What…" I bit my lip. "Hi."

Nate glanced at Liv, behind me, who began to explain. "I must've forgotten to mention it, Peps. I was in Bittersweet the other day grabbing a mocha from Nate when he told me the good news."

Beaming, Nate said, "I'm dating a *younger* woman." He gestured to Victoria in a *this one, here* kind of creepy Vanna White way. Victoria blinked—happily?—at him through her hair. "I'm officially robbing the cradle," Nate added, unnecessarily.

Shaking my head, I said, "Nope. We don't—let's not…" I pulled in a deep breath. Talking to Nate about socially-acceptable ways to word things was a constant struggle. Plus, Victoria had just graduated from Northern Washington University, the college in our hometown of Pine Crest, which meant she was probably about twenty-two. Nate was my sister's age, twenty-eight. "Six years difference between two adults is completely acceptable," I finished.

"I was so happy for them, I ended up telling Nate about our camping trip," Liv chimed in.

"And here we are." Nate sidled next to Victoria, wrapping a spider-like arm around her. The girl wasn't short, about the same height as me, but she only came up to Nate's chest, he was so tall.

We all stood there nodding silently for a few moments, looking around at the campsite. Feeling quite sure my fake smile was beginning to fade, I decided to ask some questions to fill the awkward void.

"You just graduated, right? I asked Victoria. "Any plans?"

She dipped her head. "Yeah."

We waited quietly for her to continue, but nothing came. I sighed and looked around at the trees. *So much for conversation.* Luckily, it was then—when the silence was growing thick and desperate—that I heard the guys' voices as they returned.

"Well, if you two want to unload your stuff, feel free to pull up a piece of forest." I turned and walked over to the guys, Liv hot on my heels.

Hamburger, my Boston Terrier, trotted alongside Alex, sticking close to his left heel. When she saw me, her mouth pulled into a big doggy grin and her stubby tail started to wiggle.

"Heel, Ham," Alex said, sternly.

Hammy glanced up at Alex, but *stayed with the walking master* despite her excitement, just like he'd taught her.

Frowning, I said, "Aww, you're no fun."

He smirked over the bundle of wood he held, then gave me a wink. "I'm also the reason she can walk without a leash."

The man was right, he'd worked hard with Hamburger on her walking etiquette. I appreciated it, being an absolute pushover with training—anytime she looked at me with those big brown eyes, I folded. But every once in a while, I just wanted my dog to run to me as if she hadn't seen me in years—even though it had only been half an hour.

Reading my mind, Alex said, "Go get her, Hammy," releasing the obedient dog.

Ham's muscles bunched up all at once and then she shot toward me, mouth open, tongue flying out the side. I met the black-and-white dog-bullet with wiggling fingers and kissy noises. She snorted and cut wild circles around me. Then, as if I had never existed, she pounced on a particularly large stick and began wrestling the bark from it. I laughed; I loved that dog. While she was distracted, I clipped her harness into the leash line we'd strung through our campsite.

Alex dropped the firewood next to the stone pit then went to greet Nate and Victoria. He waved and said he was glad to see them. When he came back over, Alex eyed Liv, shaking his head at her. Carson must've filled him in on the reason we had company. Nate and Victoria were nice and all. I mean, Victoria had a reputation for being the girl who didn't talk and Nate, well, he talked all too much and said all the wrong things, it seemed. But I decided their presence only made things merrier.

The sun began to set, so we busied ourselves with making a fire and getting dinner ready. Nate pulled out a hunting knife which flipped open, revealing a blade three sizes larger than we needed to help cut the hotdog packaging. In a single *snick*, the blade flicked its way straight into my nightmares.

We all shied away from the scary blade, then convinced Nate to fold it up and put it away. Once it was safely tucked back into his bag, we laughed and talked about our jobs and the quirky townspeople of Pine Crest. All the while, our rowdy neighbors played what seemed to be a full-on tournament-style drinking game.

After roasting our own hotdogs over the fire we made S'mores, contesting who had browned the most perfect "mallow" before squashing them between graham crackers and gooey chocolate. Hammy's leash turned out to be more of a weaponized clothesline than a convenient way for her to move around. Each time she ran from one end of the campsite to the other, she would either take someone's legs out from under them, nearly decapitate someone, or knock over half the supplies we had stacked on the picnic table.

So her shorter leash was wrapped around the leg of my camp chair and she was sitting in my lap by the time the sun had set, and we began telling scary stories. Carson started, with a creepy—and mostly plagiarized—tale of clowns nefariously luring children into dark spaces. Liv went next, with a chilling rendition of the time last spring when she'd been drugged, kidnapped, and almost drowned by a serial killer in our small town. I shivered and pulled Hammy close as I remembered the whole thing vividly. Victoria—not surprisingly—had nothing to say, so it was Nate who went next.

"One night in an eerie, dark forest, a group of friends decided to have a campout."

Between the chill in the air now that the sun was gone and the dry, crackly way Nate's voice mixed with the sounds of the fire, I pulled Hammy closer.

Nate continued, the orange flickering light moving across his face like something alive. "But calling them *friends* may have been going too far. One of them was an outsider, a loner. The group only invited him so they wouldn't feel bad, but everyone knew he wasn't actually welcome."

My heartbeat sped up and began to hammer in my eardrums. I widened my eyes and met Liv's mirrored expression across the fire. Her worried glances, flicking between Carson and me, told me she was wondering if Nate knew we hadn't expected him to show up this weekend.

"The outcast camper was tired of everyone always treating him like he didn't deserve to know the truth, like he didn't deserve to be part of the group. But the truth was, they were right to keep him at a distance. He was a sick and twisted soul and one night, in the middle of snores and deep, measured breaths, he snapped. Before any of them could bat an eye, he'd slashed every one of their throats." Nate swished his hand through the air. "One, two, three, four."

Liv jumped at each one. Hammy yelped as I hugged her too tight. All I could picture was the firelight reflecting off

9

the sharp edge of the switchblade I knew was tucked in Nate's bag.

Nate let his head fall back in a sinister laugh, then he put a hand on each knee. "I love camping. Well, I'm beat. I think I'm going to hit the air mattress. Goodnight!" He stood and proffered his hand toward Victoria. "M'lady?" Victoria waved goodnight as they headed toward their tent.

Audible gulps sounded around the fire: one, two, three, four.

2

Alex placed his hands behind his head as he lay back into his pillow. "So much for relaxing," he said with a sigh as the sounds of the group next to us spilled into our tent. Hammy was already snoring away, nestled in her bed in the corner of our tent.

I sat on the edge of the air mattress and pulled my socks off, shaking my head. "You almost have to laugh, really."

The group of guys in the next campsite picked that moment to let out a round of whoops and expletives. Even in the dim light of our small camp lantern, I could see Alex's jaw tighten.

"Or not…" I said with a grimace.

As if they had heard Alex's unhappy thoughts and were taking the warning seriously, our neighbors quieted down. I clicked off the lantern and snuggled into my sleeping bag next to Alex, laying my head on his chest. He wrapped an arm around me, pulling me tighter. A twig snapped outside our tent and I jumped. I could feel Alex tense next to me. My eyes scanned the tent for any shadows, especially tall, lanky, Nate-shaped ones.

"You don't really think Nate's story was about us, do you?" I whispered as a shadow danced across the fabric of our tent. It was definitely a person, and they definitely seemed to be sneaking, but it was hard to tell how far or close they were based on the distortion from the different light sources.

"We're fine, Peps." Alex sniffed out a short laugh, but I caught how he had paused for a second, waiting until the shadow had moved away before responding.

I curled my hand protectively around my neck, just in case. My eyes refused to close. When we'd arrived earlier today, I'd been reading Alex quotes from Walden as I helped him set up our tent. Now, all of the poetic lines about spending time "without any obstruction between us and the celestial bodies" and "how slight a shelter is absolutely necessary" seemed silly. All I wanted were thick walls and a locking door instead of the flimsy fabric and zipper of the tent.

As if to prove my point, the volume in the next campsite rose again. Alex cleared his throat. But this time, as our neighbors grew louder, the tone had changed. Instead of the sociable noises of a party, they quickly morphed into the sharp, biting sounds of an argument.

Swearing, shouting, and the occasional "oomph" of a punch rang through the air. Alex and I sat up. His expression narrowed. He flipped back his sleeping bag and swung his feet onto the tent floor. Hamburger watched Alex, poised to follow.

"Where are you going?" I hissed.

"To break up whatever drunken fight is happening next door."

I grabbed his arm. "Uh, no you aren't. You're not leaving me and Ham alone in here. Plus, I don't want you getting in the middle of that. We're on a relaxing vacation. Your first away from the force, might I remind you. You're not on duty this week." I moved my hand to his shoulder. "Let the rangers take care of it."

Alex's chest expanded as he pulled in a deep breath. The yelling ebbed and seemed to die out. After a second, Alex nodded, exhaling. "Okay. You're right."

We settled back. I was happy he'd listened to me, but suspected his presence in our tent had much more to do with the fight coming to an end than that I'd asked him to stay. Either way, I snuggled up to him, laid my head back onto his chest, and tried to get some sleep.

———

I FELT like a tree had fallen on me the next morning. Between Alex stirring at every noise outside our tent, Hammy growling at what seemed like nothing—but could've been Nate coming to slit our throats with his unnecessarily large knife—and the sounds from our noisy neighbors, I think I'd gotten something like twenty-seven minutes of sleep.

Alex rubbed at his eyes, and I noticed they were red and bloodshot just like I was sure mine were. Even Hammy looked like she'd had a rough night as she snorted and flopped back into her bed, hiding her head under one paw.

"Good morning," I croaked, my voice sounding gravelly and just as worse for wear as my body felt.

"Remains to be seen," Alex answered, making his side of the air mattress. My boyfriend was a bit of a neat freak. He eyed my still-rumpled sleeping bag.

"Not today," I said with a groan. "I don't have the energy to pretend I'm tidy. I need coffee, stat. Though, I'm not sure the instant stuff we brought is going to cut it after last night. I'm definitely not cut out to live the simple life like Thoreau."

Chuckling, Alex said, "Well, Thoreau lived by a quiet pond and didn't have wild neighbors keeping him up until the wee hours of the morning."

"True." I yawned, unzipped the door to our tent, and the three of us stumbled outside into the bright morning light.

Liv and Carson were just staggering out of their tent, and they blinked blearily at us. It looked like we weren't the only ones up half the night. Carson's chin-length brown hair was usually kind of an endearing mess, but Liv's normally sleek blond hair sat in some sort of rat's nest on the top of her head, making my hand move to check my hair.

Flinching at the frizziness my fingers met, I decided not to further investigate. Carson rubbed his neck, and we stood there yawning for a moment. Alex grabbed Hammy's leash and walked her around the edge of the campsite to do her business.

My attention turned to the next campsite. Bodies littered the ground as if a plague had hit the campsite abruptly. The only signs of life were the snores and occasional movements of the guys. They hadn't even attempted to put up tents, but had thrown sleeping bags onto the ground, fallen asleep in camp chairs or on the picnic table. A leg hung out of one the truck beds parked next to their site.

"Looks like they eventually passed out." Liv wrinkled her nose at the sight.

"More than I can say for any of us." I turned toward Nate's tent, remembering our rowdy neighbors hadn't been the only reason we'd had a hard time getting to sleep.

I jumped as I noticed Victoria and Nate already sitting around the campfire.

"Good morning," Nate said, holding up a honey-colored Bittersweet mug.

Victoria gave a sheepish wave.

I was about to wave back when a sharp elbow landed square in my gut, making me double over. Liv was a blond streak as she shoved past us, to the fire. But when I saw what had caught her interest, I understood the rush.

Next to Nate sat a portable version of the espresso machine he used at Bittersweet, syrups, milk and other coffee house paraphernalia. A small generator hummed next to him. Sad visions of gross instant coffee disappeared and I raced forward, stopping just behind Liv.

"Nate, you brought—?" It was as if Liv couldn't make herself utter the word until she was sure.

"To share?" I asked, eagerly, fingers clutching Liv's arm as we waited for his response.

Nate dipped his head, his thin lips curling up into a satisfied smile. "But of course, I brought enough to share with all of my friends."

I held my breath for a second, glancing at Liv. The tone he used when he said "friends" made my stomach churn, but I really needed good coffee after the night we had. Liv's eyes narrowed for a second as she seemed to go through the same thought process. *But his story was about slitting throats, not poisoning the campers...* my tired, caffeine-deprived mind rationalized.

"He spent all week perfecting the gear," Victoria said, speaking her first complete sentence since she'd arrived yesterday. "Was even up tinkering with it a few times last night."

Liv and I froze, watching her, waiting for anything else

to come out of her mouth—a warning maybe—but that seemed to be it.

"Well I'm in," I said, plopping into the seat next to Nate.

"Make that two," Liv said, sitting to my right.

I caught Alex and Carson shaking their heads at us from the corner of my eye, but I didn't care because moments later Nate was handing me a steaming mug of delicious-smelling coffee.

"Kanpai," I said, holding my mug toward Liv as I pronounced the Japanese version of cheers.

"Yamas," she said, picking Greek in our continued efforts to bring culture to our drinking, both alcoholic and non.

Pulling my mug back to me, I closed my eyes and breathed in the cinnamon-scented steam for a few moments before taking my first sip. Even the smell of the coffee seemed to take the edge off my too-little-sleep headache. From the first taste, I was in heaven. It was frothy; cinnamon and vanilla flavors danced with a light sweetness and then the smooth taste of life-giving, energy-providing coffee hit me.

"Best. Day. Ever," I said, keeping my eyes closed, taking another sip.

"More like Nate saves the day," Liv said next to me.

When I finally opened my eyes, Nate was watching us, beaming. Alex and Carson, upon seeing us still alive, seemed to make up their minds about the coffee being safe and asked Nate for their own mugs.

After our coffee and a quick breakfast of granola bars and apples, we packed some lunch and water into backpacks and headed out for a hike.

Thanks to Nate's coffee, the effects of our sleepless night were sufficiently hidden underneath layers of caffeine and sugar. The sun shone brightly through the tall pine trees, and a cool mountain breeze brushed through the forest. I clipped Hamburger's backpack around her middle and snapped her retractable leash on to the hook between her shoulder blades.

With one last glance over at our still soundly sleeping neighbors, we locked up our valuables then started out toward the trail nearest to our campsite.

Each long pull of fresh air through my nose seemed to wake me up even more, invigorating any remaining sleepiness dormant inside. I smiled at the soft crunch of our boots on the dried pine needles lining the trail. Hammy's collar jangled quietly, mixing with the musical bird songs echoing around us in the tall pines.

Our group snaked silently through the trees for a few minutes. Alex and Hammy stuck with me in the lead, and Nate and Victoria brought up the caboose behind Liv and Carson. Conversations began to spring up as people pushed ahead or fell back, our group finding a nice fluid arrangement as we hiked.

When we'd walked for a good ten minutes away from the camp, I leaned down and unclipped Hammy's lead. We hadn't seen a soul since the campsite, and she was good enough at listening without her leash, especially now with all of Alex's training. She looked back at Alex when she realized the leash was off and he gave her a quick nod.

"Stay close, Ham."

The dog snorted and then pranced in a tight circle around the group as we continued to walk. Today's hike wasn't so much about elevation as the destination. There was a beautiful waterfall a few miles from where we were camping I thought might make a great lunch destination.

As we walked, I thought of the many times I'd been

camping with my family. Dad and I would always disappear for hours, wandering the woods, quoting Thoreau, and drinking in the peaceful sounds of the forest.

"Heaven is under our feet as well as over our heads," I said, quoting one of Dad's favorite lines.

Everyone seemed to settle, relaxing into the wild around us. Even Alex, who I knew thought the author was highly overrated, nodded. Finally, away from our noisy neighbors and the bustle of the campground, I started to feel the peace envelop me too. The smoky scent of campfires was slowly being replaced by the sweet smell of wildflowers as we headed toward the ridge. Everything seemed perfect.

Simple. Quiet. Thoughtfu—

Hammy's furious barking cut through my focus, making my eyes fly open in surprise, just in time to see her race into a bush at the side of the trail. "Ham, no," I yelled after her. To no avail.

I looked to Alex. She always listened to Alex. His face darkened as he called to her. "Hammy, heel."

Nothing. My forehead creased in worry as her barking only became more intense. We ran over to where she'd disappeared. Alex parted the woody branches of two large rhododendrons and we slipped through to a small clearing.

And froze.

Hammy stopped barking as she saw us, her tongue lolling to the side happily. She sat down, almost as if saying, "Oh good, you're here. Look what I found."

My gaze crept past my small dog to the boot, to the leg, and then the body. The man was lying on this stomach, his face turned to one side. And he was still. Stomach dropping, I sank to a kneeling position, calling Hammy to me, away from the man. Now the dog trotted happily over to me, letting me gather her up in my arms, snapping the leash back on her just in case.

Once Alex made sure I had a hold of her, he held up a hand. It was then that I noticed the rest of our group had followed us into the clearing. They were staring, eyes wide at the body as Alex stepped closer.

I could see Alex's jaw tighten as he knelt next to the man and peered around at the face, hidden behind a mop of short, curly brown hair.

My stomach dropped as I recognized that hair.

I waited for Alex to check for a pulse or shake the man awake, but he didn't. Instead he cleared his throat and looked back at us, shaking his head. I stood and took a few steps to the right.

And that's when I saw it—the reason Alex didn't bother to check for a pulse—the sticky blood pooling below his throat, coating the dried grass in the clearing. I hugged Hammy tight to me as Alex stood and backed up until he was standing next to me.

"I'm sorry," I whispered.

His brows furrowed.

"I should've let you go out and break up the fight last night," I continued, pointing to the two embroidered symbols on the guy's left sleeve. While I didn't know the design on the left—it looked like the top portion of a star—next to it was a marmot, our local university's mascot.

In addition to the sweatshirt, I remembered that curly brown hair.

Recognition lifted Alex's features and he sighed. The man lying facedown, dead in the forest was definitely one of the keg-stand crew from the campsite next to us.

3

I'd assumed the fight we'd overheard last night was a simple drunken brawl, something that would fizzle out after the guys were pulled apart and their friends intervened.

I glanced at the blood beading on the blades of grass.

A line from the beginning of Walden came to me. Thoreau had said, "Men hit only what they aim at." This was no accident. Someone had wanted this guy dead, and they'd made sure their aim was true.

"I don't have any reception," Alex said, as he frowned at his phone. "Any of you?"

After a quick check, we each shook our heads; none of us had service this far out either.

Alex's jaw tightened as he looked around. "We're going to have to go back to the campground and tell the rangers, then. I can stay here and make sure nothing disturbs the body."

Mind abuzz, Alex's words didn't seem to register. My gaze tiptoed over to the man's throat, to the very edge of a long cut in his skin. Shivering, I had to look away. Then it hit me. Nate's scary story. Slitting throats—well, throat, in this case. Nate's large switchblade. I'd been unable to sleep half the night worrying about Nate's terrible tale coming true, and in a way, it had. Did the creepy barista have something to do with this?

I'd gotten warm during our short hike and had tied my light, summer sweatshirt onto my waist. Now that we had stopped, and with what we'd found, I shimmied back into it, relishing the way the cotton settled on my skin, making me feel wrapped up and safe. Sort of.

Attention settling on Nate, I noticed he didn't seem worried, or sad, or even all that disturbed. But really, just because he'd happened to choose a scary story involving slitting throats didn't automatically mean he was responsible for all throat slitting in the surrounding area. Right? Still I didn't really want to end up in his group, if we did decide to split up.

Carson spoke up, breaking up my paranoid thoughts. "Want me to stay with you?" he asked Alex.

"We really only need one person to stay," Alex said, looking to Carson. "I need you to get everyone back safely and let the rangers know where to find me." He was in full cop mode now, serious and all about the task ahead.

Carson shook his head. "It should be you going to talk to the rangers, Alex. They'll listen to a cop way more than me. I'll stay. You get these guys back."

Alex agreed and started giving Carson instructions on what to do and say when the rangers showed up.

"I'm not leaving you here alone," Liv said.

He put a hand on each of her shoulders. "I'll be fine, babe. Please go."

She sighed reluctantly, but nodded, and then we were off. Liv linked her arm through mine, and we pulled close as we walked away.

I waited to let Hammy down until we were a good few minutes away from the body. A shiver spiked up my spine at the thought that, if Hamburger hadn't been off leash, we would've probably walked right by the body, unaware of the small clearing just feet from the main path. It was hard not to wish I'd kept the dog on her leash, though I hated to think of what other animal might've found the body if Hammy hadn't. Had the killer been counting on that very possibility?

We walked back to the campgrounds in silence, the weight of what happened dragging us down as if we'd pulled the dead guy along after us.

"I'm sure we don't all need to go report this. I'll go back to the campsite with Victoria and rustle up another round of coffees. I think we could all use a bit of a pick-up after that business," Nate said as the tents came into view.

My paranoid mind spent a second wondering if Nate was trying to get out of talking to the ranger for other reasons—guilt-shaped ones—but another cup of good coffee sounded too perfect to pass up. Splitting up, the rest of us headed for the rangers' offices at the entrance to the campground.

Alex held a hand up as we approached the small building. Liv and I stayed outside with Hammy while he entered. I could see him reach in his pocket, pulling out his badge. Hamburger snuffled around on the ground as Liv wrapped her arms around herself, her face looking pale and wracked with concern.

Also feeling like I'd been hit in the gut with one of my big hiking boots, I tried to calm myself down. I listened to the birds chirping in the sunlit treetops, a bass line of buzzing crickets providing the background to their songs.

A few minutes later, the door swung open with a squeak,

and I glanced up to see Alex. His forehead was furrowed, but he gave me a somber nod. It was taken care of.

"I'm going to stay here and wait for the sheriff. They said he's only about fifteen minutes away. They're going to hold everyone in the campground for questioning for a few hours, but we can start packing at least. You two can head back to the site and get started if you want."

I placed a hand on his arm and squeezed it tight. I wanted to pull him close, ask him to wrap his arms tight around me until I forgot the blood, the body. But I also didn't want to seem like a wimp. Alex was focused on his job as a police officer right now. Even though he wasn't in uniform, I could see the change in him.

But the faster he could fill the sheriff in on what we knew, the sooner we could get out of here. There was a quick pang of frustration at the idea of cutting our vacation short. This was the last real week of my summer vacation from grad school and the one week my employee in the bookstore could cover for me. I'd been working my butt off for the last year, owning a shop in town while keeping up with my classes at the university.

And I wasn't the only one who needed the break. Liv, Carson, and Alex had all started new jobs since graduating last year. We were all overworked, needing the "absolute Freedom and Wildness of nature" to restore us just like Thoreau.

I recognized the same tight regret about leaving in Liv's eyes as she looked over at me, but she nodded. There was no way we could stay. If I'd thought last night was scary, I couldn't imagine another with an actual murderer on the loose.

"Okay, see you back there," I said to Alex.

Liv and I left him, making our way back to our site,

glancing back to see two of the three rangers clomp out of the office and head toward the trail, walkie talkies at the ready, while Alex waited for the sheriff. I turned back toward our campsite, toward the promise of more caffeine to give me energy for packing and an unexpected trip home. But when we arrived, it appeared I was going to have some competition for that coffee.

Crowded around Nate and Victoria were five of the guys from the next campsite. From their puffy eyes and disheveled hair, they appeared to have just woken up. I simultaneously felt a pang of pity for them—by the looks of it, they didn't yet know one of their friends was lying dead in the woods—and fear for us—based on the fight we heard last night, one of these guys could very well be the throat slitter. Nate was handing out disposable cups of coffee. The guys' faces practically lit up as they took their first sips.

What was Nate doing inviting potential murderers over for coffee? Should we tell them about their friend?

My mind frantically went over what Alex would do in this situation. Would he say something? Would he try to investigate first? Also, even if I did *want* to tell them, what would I say? I wasn't practiced in breaking news like this to someone, let alone a whole group of someones.

Inwardly groaning, I settled in an open seat on one of the logs farthest away from our company. It definitely wouldn't do to start packing our things up while they were sitting here. That would surely illicit questions. No, for now we needed to pretend everything was normal.

From the stiff way Liv sat at the fire pit, I'd say I wasn't the only one who was feeling the awkwardness of the situation. She grimaced, and her body scrunched in tight as her face seemed to follow those emoji scales for discomfort they hang in hospitals. Hamburger even seemed wary, sticking close to me when a few of our neighbors tried to call her over. Overly friendly by nature —my dog was used to hanging out at my bookshop all day, customers coming and going constantly—it was quite unusual for Hammy to pull the shy card. Could she smell the killer's scent? Recognize it on the body she'd helped us find?

My eyes were narrowed and decidedly shifty as they roamed over our visitors.

Two more college guys schlepped themselves over during the time it took Nate to get mugs into all of our hands. Once I had coffee in front of me again, I began to breathe a little easier.

"Anyone seen James?" one of the keg-stand crew asked, glancing back at their now-empty campground.

My easy breath caught in my throat. Guilt clenched its terrible fingers around my gut as I wondered whether or not to say anything. Liv whimpered, looking like a strong eight on the discomfort scale.

"Hey, you okay?" one of the guys asked Liv. His attention turned to me and from the worry which met me in his eyes, I guessed I didn't look much better than Liv.

"Uh, we're… fine. We just…" I trailed off, not knowing how to finish.

Nate cleared his throat. "*We're* fine. But I'm afraid we have some bad news for you."

All at once, I made my decision. We definitely were *not* trained to tell these guys this level of bad news. Plus, the sheriff was on his way. I just needed to keep Nate quiet until Alex got back. He would know what to do.

I glanced over at Liv, who choked on her coffee then coughed into her sleeve. I pressed my lips together. I made wide eyes at Nate and tried to shake my head without our guests noticing. But they were leaning in close, ready to hear the continuation of Nate's statement.

"This coffee is actually decaf," I blurted out, shoulders bunching up like a bad pair of underwear. "Sorry!" I laughed too loud and tried to catch Nate's attention.

Confused by my reaction, the guys just blinked down at their coffee, some taking more tentative sips after my outburst.

After a moment, another guy said, "Come to think of it, I haven't seen James since last night."

The college guys scanned the group, as if this James might be hiding in plain sight.

"You know how he gets sometimes, though," a guy with a reddish beard said. "He's always disappearing when he gets drunk."

"Grady's right, he's probably in a bush somewhere sleeping it off. Remember when we found him on a bench on campus the morning after his birthday?"

They laughed and nodded, most of their worries settling at this reminder, unlike those of us who knew the truth.

This was terrible. Sitting here, knowing their friend was dead and not being able to tell them was turning out to be a super weird form of torture. Liv looked green; she stared down at her coffee as if it actually *was* decaf. Even Victoria seemed like she wanted to say something to make it all better.

If I couldn't tell them, maybe I could at least get some information for Alex and the sheriff. Remembering the fight we'd overheard, I watched our guests closely for any signs of guilt. Half of them shook their heads, appearing confused, but what interested me was the other half. They sat up straight, muttered something unintelligible, or looked down at their coffees. They knew something.

"I don't think this is one of his normal disappearing acts." A blond guy across from me glared at a large brutish dude next to him. "I think it has more to do with—"

"Shut it, Kevin." The brute curled his fingers around his paper coffee cup so tightly I worried the thing might burst and waste precious coffee in a messy spray.

Kevin put his hands up. "Just sayin' I think you went too far this time, Matt," Kevin continued, holding his gaze on Matt.

I leaned forward.

Matt glared. "James is a big boy, he was the one who decided to take off in the middle of the night. Plus, I searched for him for a good half hour. I bet he left." The big guy shrugged.

"But his truck's still here," a scrawny, dark-haired guy pointed out, worry lacing his words as he motioned to the grouping of the three trucks parked in the next campsite.

A few of the guys began whispering.

"I don't know where he is." Matt shoved his words through mostly clenched teeth. He placed a hand over his heart. "Swear." He watched the blond guy as he took a long drink of his coffee.

My pulse quickened. With that comment from Kevin, the cut on Matt's lip and the bruise forming over his left eye, it was easy enough to see he was the one who'd gotten in the fight we overheard last night. *I searched for him*, Matt had said. What if he *had* in fact found James in the woods last night? Found him and slit his throat. I could see Liv's fingers curl tighter, gripping the log she sat on as she listened to the conversation, reassuring me I wasn't the only one noticing Matt wore guilt as obviously as his hangover.

The guilt I was pretty sure about, but what he was guilty of still seemed up for question.

Intriguing as Matt and his apparent fight with poor James was, I knew the most obvious suspect was rarely the guilty party. If every one of their friends witnessed Matt and James get in a fight, and then saw Matt head out into the woods in search of James, the guy would have to be a complete idiot to commit a crime. Of course he'd be everyone's first suspect.

Hammy chose that moment to venture forward, sniffing the newcomers and stepping cautiously as she inched closer to the nearest guy. He reached down and patted her head, scratching behind her ears. Her body relaxed and her tongue lolled out of her mouth as she began to pant and smile up at him. Seemingly reassured that these people were okay, she began to make the rounds, leaning up against each new leg, hoping for a pat or a scratch.

Being tired and hungover aside—Hammy's cuteness wasn't something easily ignored—soon she had most of the guys vying for her attention. When she reached Matt, I tensed, watching and waiting. But my shoulders quickly settled as he smiled and patted her side.

Just as I was letting my guard down, however, I heard a low growl roll out of Hamburger. It wasn't directed at Matt, however. She was staring straight at Kevin, the blond guy who'd accused Matt just minutes ago.

Kevin tried to put his hand down and call her over, but Hammy only sniffed the air, sneezed, and then ran back to me, barking at him the whole way. Kevin's face turn red and his gaze became shifty. Had Hammy smelled something on him or just sensed things were amiss? She'd only growled at a handful of people since I'd adopted her almost two years earlier. If she was feeling weird about Kevin, there was something up with the guy. It didn't escape me that he'd been the first to point a finger at Matt when James was discovered missing.

Often the first to lay blame was the real culprit, right?

Quiet settled over the group, and even here in the fresh outdoor air, it felt stifling.

One of the guys continued to glance to his left toward their campsite every few seconds. He had brown hair, but a reddish beard. His facial hair was on the long side, but well groomed. While his body language definitely made him appear relaxed, I was sure he hadn't dropped the conversation about James. The way he kept checking gave me the distinct impression he was waiting for someone to show up at their campsite.

And when the guys had drained their coffees and were just starting to look alive again, someone did.

A forest-green sheriff's SUV pulled to a slow stop next to their line of cars. The faces of our visitors either drained to pale or darkened with worry as they noticed the vehicle and the tall man stepping out of it. Alex climbed out of the passenger side.

After saying something to the sheriff, Alex pointed to our campfire. They both headed our way.

Clearing his throat, the sheriff said, "Which of you are from the next campsite over?"

The keg-stand crew stood, some on noticeably wobbly legs.

"Mind if I have a word with you boys?" I heard the sheriff ask.

As they responded in the affirmative and followed him back to their site, I closed my eyes, knowing the bad news they were about to receive.

4

L iv pulled her shoulders up high in discomfort as she watched our neighboring campers receive the unfortunate news about their friend.

"Ugh. I don't think I can watch this." She stood and then wandered away. "I'm going to start packing.

Nate and Victoria wandered toward their tent as well, and as much as I agreed with Liv—this was awkward and awful—I found myself unable to look away. There was still a possibility that one of them had killed their friend. I had a feeling watching their reactions might give me some insight into who could be guilty.

Just then, Alex plopped down on the log across from me, blocking my view of our neighbors. About to scowl at him, I stopped myself when he moved slightly to one side.

"Can you still see?" he asked in a low voice.

Glancing up, I nodded. "Yeah, if you stay just like that."

Alex winked. "This way it looks like you're just talking to me."

I smiled, glad he wasn't mad I'd been doing a little investigating. "The sheriff asked you to help, then?"

Features tightening, he sighed. "Actually, the opposite. He made it pretty clear I was well outside of my jurisdiction. But that doesn't mean we can't make observations." Alex trained his eyes on mine, keeping his back to the other camp. "Who are our suspects?"

Whispering, I filled him in on what I'd noticed while he was with the sheriff. "I'm watching Matt, the biggest one behind you. According to the group, he and James got into a big fight last night. I also get a weird vibe from the one with the reddish beard. And then there's Kevin, the blond guy. He was the first to point fingers."

"How are they taking it?" Alex asked, leaning forward.

Pretending to look at him, I observed the varying reactions to the terrible news.

"Matt is standing back. His arms are crossed and he's all tight: face, body, eyes. He looks upset, in his own way. He reminds me of... never mind, it's silly."

"What?" Alex asked.

I focused on his face instead of looking past it. "He reminds me of Brooklyn, when she's been throwing a fit about something and then she realizes she's wrong, but she's made too big of a deal to let go just yet, so she stomps around mad for a while longer just so it doesn't look like she gave in," I said. Alex nodded, having spent quite a bit of time with my five-year old niece.

"Kevin is interesting, too. Hammy started growling at him. You know she never does that," I said. I scooped my dog into my lap and then glanced over at the guys. "He almost seems like he's playing a part. As if he's auditioning for the part of 'devastated friend number two' and studied exactly how someone should react when hearing news of this kind. He paced for a while, shook his head, cried a bit, and now he's sitting in a chair with his head in his hands."

Alex sighed. "Without knowing how close these guys actually were to James, it's hard to tell if that's a real reaction or not. Do the others seem to be noticing Kevin, watching him especially?"

Understanding what Alex was asking me to check for, I said, "No, maybe it's not an act, then. Maybe this is just how he always is."

"Or maybe everyone else is too stunned by the news they just heard." Alex shrugged. "I don't like how Ham reacted to him, though, so I definitely don't want to discount the possibility that something's up." He reached forward and scrunched Hammy's face with both hands just like she loved.

I nodded. "Redbeard, I think his name might be Grady or Brady, looks like he's about to puke." I grimaced. "Like, seriously, the guy is gree—oh gross."

Alex frowned as he heard the sound of Redbeard throwing up into the bushes behind us. Hammy's ears swiveled and she tilted her head.

"Could be shock," I said.

"Could be guilt, too. Disbelief he actually went through with it," Alex said.

Clearing my throat, I focused squarely on Alex. "True. Well, should we start packing up?" I asked as I stood. I was anxious to get away from this place and get this whole ordeal behind us.

Alex stood next to me and then wrapped his arm around my shoulder, pulling me tight liked I'd wanted him to earlier. He planted a kiss on my forehead, and we turned toward the tent to start the process of leaving.

Thirty minutes later, Carson had returned and the rest of us were all packed, besides our tents. Unsure what to do next, we stood awkwardly. The neighbors were still being questioned by the sheriff and his deputy who had taken a break from helping the rangers question the rest of the campers. And while I knew they probably wouldn't even notice us, it just felt crass to start shoving everything in our cars to leave while they were going through so many terrible emotions.

"Maybe we can wait for a half hour or so? Just until they start packing up, too?" I suggested.

The group nodded and we congregated around the fire pit again. "Heads up," Liv said. "Sheriff's coming over here."

Alex's face darkened. He left to meet the sheriff at the edge of our camp.

They looked pretty similar, actually. Both tall, both dark haired, both wearing the serious scowls I'd come to associate with cops. The sheriff had a good decade on Alex, though —and he was wearing a hat which appeared more "cowboy" than anything I could ever picture my boyfriend donning. The hat was just the beginning of their differences, too. As Alex had mentioned, instead of appearing grateful another law enforcement officer was on the scene so early, the man seemed bothered by Alex's presence.

Alex moved aside and motioned toward our fire pit. "Here's our whole group, this was everyone who was on the hike when we found the body. We were all together," Alex told him when they got close enough.

His badge read "Langley" and his face read "unamused." Clearing his throat, the sheriff held up a hand. He eyed me and then looked back to Alex. "I'd prefer to get statements individually, rather than as a group."

I swallowed the scoff climbing up my throat. Separately? As if we might be hiding something? As if we were somehow suspects in this whole ordeal?

Movement in the surrounding campsites caught my eye. There were rangers and a few other officers walking around with notebooks, getting people's information and asking questions, it appeared.

Alex appeared to be equally confused by Sheriff Langley's implication. Regardless, he understood his rank and put his hands up. "You're in charge."

The sheriff flipped a page in his notebook. I could've sworn he muttered something along the lines of, "And don't you forget it, buddy boy."

Feeling so far removed from my precious Thoreau-inspired quiet woodsy getaway, and a little too much like I was in some sort of wooded *West Side Story*—I mean, come on... buddy boy?—I stepped forward hoping to break the tension.

"I can go first if you'd like," I said, handing Hammy's leash off to Alex and giving him an "I'll be fine" wink before turning back to face the sheriff.

Langley's gaze landed on me and scanned me up and down like I imagined he would when presented with a new case file. Then his attention lingered on my body at little too long. I shivered. This case file was only wearing a T-shirt and cutoffs, wishing she had something to cover up with super quick.

He shrugged and said, "Ladies first." Without a thread of actual chivalry, he led me over to the picnic table away from the fire pit.

As I sat at the table, Alex settled on one of the logs around the pit, perched like a hawk. Hammy jumped into his lap and settled in for a nap. Satisfied my boyfriend was as comfortable as he was going to get, I focused on my interview.

"And your name is?" Sheriff Langley asked.

"Pepper Brooks."

The sheriff's eyes narrowed a little at my name. What? Did he think I was lying?

He jotted down my name, then looked back at me. "Why are you here?" he asked, voice cold, gaze harsh.

"Camping with friends. Vacation."

I almost expected him to snort and accuse me of lying. Instead he said, "Tell me about finding the body earlier."

Starting with last night, I tried to slip a few clues I'd noticed with my story, knowing this guy wasn't likely to take input from me if he didn't even want to hear from Alex. I'd managed to mention the fight we'd overheard as well as the figure I'd seen sneaking around by our tent just before. If Sheriff Langley noticed I was making any conjectures about the case, he didn't let on, so I went on to describe Hammy finding the body.

"His throat was obviously cut and there was a lot of blood." I swallowed, taking a second to remember what else I'd noticed at the scene. "I recognized seeing him the day before, because of his curly brown hair. Then I noticed a marmot stitched onto the sleeve of his sweatshirt. That's my school. Grad school, that is." I glanced up and smiled.

Langley watched me, his face deadpan.

I shook my head. "Oh, and there was something else next to the marmot. It was like the top part of a star… I don't know. I feel like I've seen it before, but I can't remember what it means."

After finishing the sentence he was writing, the sheriff looked over his shoulder at the other campsite, as if searching for something he hadn't seen when he'd been over there.

"And then none of us had service, so we left Carson while we hiked back to tell the rangers." I rushed through the last part of my story, ready for this whole thing to be over.

Langley scanned his notes and then nodded. "I'll let you know if I have any other questions. Can you send over the next person in your group?"

I padded back over to the group and Liv stood up, volunteering to go next. Once she was seated across from Langley, I settled next to Alex.

Hamburger was sound asleep, her unmistakable snoring grumbling out from her little body. Alex smiled despite his rigid posture as I tucked myself next to him on the log, slipping my arm through his and resting my head on his shoulder.

"How'd it go?" Alex asked instead of saying, "I hate that guy" like I'd expected him to.

"Fine."

"You tell him any of your theories?"

I shot him an incredulous look. "You really think Sheriff I-don't-need-your-help is going to listen to my theories?"

Chuckling, Alex said, "Point taken. So you slid them in as if they were just part of your story?"

"You know me too well."

"Not possible," he said, wrapping his arm around me. "I know you just the right amount."

And even with the sun directly above, wrapped in Alex's embrace, I felt another shiver pass over me.

5

Alex held his hand out to the sheriff as he stood a while later, signaling the end of the questioning. He was the last one in our group to explain how we came across the body. They walked over to where the rest of us sat around the remains of last night's fire.

"Well, I have your contact information. I'll be in touch if we need anything more from you folks." Sheriff Langley perched his cowboy hat back on top of his head, having removed it during questioning—possibly just so he could better furrow his brow at everything we said.

"So you don't need us to stay around any longer?" Alex asked, crossing his arms over his chest.

The sheriff shrugged. "Nope. You're free to leave. Nothing to worry about here. It's probably just an animal attack, to be honest. There are mountain lions all over the place up here. But we'll have to wait for the medical examiner's report to be sure."

I blinked, swallowing a scoff as the sheriff gave us a nod and walked back over to his deputy who was ushering the college guys into two sheriffs' SUVs.

"What?" I whispered when he was out of earshot. "There's no way a mountain lion did that unless it was holding a knife." I turned to Alex.

Alex looked after the two vehicles, pulling away, leaving the next campground quiet and empty. "I don't know, Pepper. The guy was on his stomach; we didn't see the full cut on his neck. It *could've* been claw marks."

"Right, because mountain lions regularly trot around the woods at night, slicing people's throats open and then leaving them without any other injuries." I crossed my arms over my chest.

He sighed.

"Alex, they don't. A mountain lion would use its teeth, first of all, plus there wasn't a paw print near the body. I can't believe Sheriff Langley is blowing off a *murder* like this. One of those guys could have killed their friend."

"Well, it looks like he's taking them in for questioning, at least," Liv pointed out, having heard my worries.

"Does that mean anything?" Carson asked Alex.

"Technically they should only take people in for questioning if they have evidence enough to believe they're suspects," he answered. "Though, he doesn't seem to particularly care for going by the book."

I scoffed. "That's the understatement of the year. I think Sheriff Langley is either really lazy or really bad at his job."

"Like the striped snake," Alex mused, repeating Thoreau's metaphor for those who walk through life unaware, completely obtuse.

Smiling wide, I said, "See? *Walden* isn't all bad, right?"

Alex tipped his head reluctantly.

"I don't know what you two are talking about, but that sheriff was awful. Can you believe he asked Carson if he had a scrunchie he could use to pull the hair out of his face?" Liv asked, still fuming. "I like your hair like this."

At the mention, Carson ran a hand through his shaggy brown locks, pushing them back and out of his face. "Thanks, babe, but I don't really care what an uptight jerk thinks. I'm on vacation. Plus, I probably *could* use a haircut." He shrugged.

"And he refused my offer of a fresh cup of french roast." Nate shook his head. To him, that was just as bad as a personal insult.

I put both hands up. "The guy is literally the worst. I kinda wish Mags was here. I feel like she could've put him in his place."

My older sister had followed in our mother's litigious footsteps, and even though she'd taken some time off for her kids and had yet to finish her law degree, she was already as fierce an arguer as I'd met since… well, our mom.

Liv's face darkened after a second. "Speaking of Maggie…"

"Oh, right." I wrinkled my nose. My sister and her family were supposed to join us tonight, but now we were leaving… They wouldn't be leaving for another couple of hours, but if I could save my busy sis some unnecessary packing, it would be worth it to let her know now. Standing, I said, "I should give her a call."

Out of habit, I reached for my cell phone, only to remember it was about as helpful as a brick out here in the woods.

"Touché, Mr. Thoreau," I mumbled to myself as I slipped it back into my pocket. Even though the writer had died way before cellular technology was developed, I had a feeling he would've despised the things.

"There's a phone at the ranger's office. They might let

you use it," Carson said, having noticed my lack of luck with my cell.

Liv moved to stand. "Want me to come with you?"

A line from Walden stuck in my memory. "I love to be alone. I never found the companion that was so companionable as solitude." And while I didn't agree completely—I loved being with my friends almost as much as I loved sitting alone with a good book—a little solitude didn't sound like a bad idea, especially after the morning we'd had.

I waved a dismissive hand toward her. "I'll be fine." I wrapped Hammy's leash around my hand twice and nudged her awake where she was sleeping by my feet. As tired as she seemed, I had a feeling she would appreciate the walk. "I'll take Ham with me."

Alex cleared his throat. "No way I'm letting you go alone. Hamburger couldn't protect you against a butterfly."

The man had a point. A quiet walk ala Thoreau sounded nice, but Henry David hadn't had a throat-slicing murderer sneaking around his woods. I conceded and Alex followed me.

Our feet crunched on the pine needles littering the road as we followed it through the campground. Hammy snuffled along the edges of the path, stopping short each time she smelled something interesting—which was often. There were many empty sites now, evident as I walked closer to the ranger's office. After the officers had come around to question everyone, people must've high-tailed it home. I wondered how soon we'd be able to get on the road.

Pulling in what felt like it would be my last breath of fresh, mountain air, I had to admit—murderer aside—I was going to miss the woods. Alex walked silently next to me, seeming to appreciate the quiet as well. I linked my arm with his and pulled myself a little closer.

A bird sang out a delightful tune somewhere to my right, and I closed my eyes for a second. Pushing thoughts of the murder out of my mind, I tried to relax. I needed to let go of the awful tightness I'd been holding on to since finding James's body. Warm rays landed on my face, and I blinked my eyes open.

The sun was almost completely overhead, heating up the earth as the day progressed. A light, perfect breeze seemed to whoosh by, providing just the right amount of relief from the heat, which was greatly lessened by the tall, stately pines which allowed only slivers and shafts of golden light to bathe the soft forest floor. Other than the birds—and the occasional sound of other campers—there was the ever-present hum of the mountains surrounding everything.

What was that sound they made? Probably just the wind racing past their craggy peaks and jutting precipices, but since I was a little girl, it had always felt like the mountains themselves were making the noise, reminding us they were here, would always be.

As we rounded the bend and the little office came into view, one of the rangers stood outside. Recognizing Alex, he tipped his head in a hello.

"You go inside, I'm going to talk to him for a few," Alex said.

I nodded, letting my arm fall away from his as he broke away and walked toward the man as I walked inside. Old wooden stairs creaked as I scaled the four steps up to the squeaky door, which alerted the rangers of customers just as the small bell hanging over my door at the bookshop did. Hammy and I walked farther inside, discovering a middle-aged woman tucked behind an old wooden counter.

"Afternoon," she said with a broad smile.

"Do you perhaps have a phone I could use?" I squinted one eye. "My cell is just about useless out here."

"Absolutely." She pointed to an old, avocado-colored rotary telephone sitting on the counter to her right. "If you don't mind doing a bit of time traveling."

"Not at all." I stepped down to the end of the counter, picking Hammy up so she wouldn't eat something odd off the ground while I was distracted.

"Ohmigosh, your dog is adorable." The ranger stood to get a better view of Ham.

"You wanna hold her?" I asked jokingly, but then thought about it. "Actually, that might be helpful. She can get into trouble if I'm not watching her."

The woman nodded, reached forward, and pulled Hammy away from me. Ham began licking the woman's face, saying hello. I laughed and then focused on my call.

Dialing Maggie's number on the rotary took a while, but it made me want to giggle in delight. The dial tone buzzed in my ear as I waited.

"Hello?"

"Mags, it's Pepper. Sorry for the weird number, but there's no service up here. I'm using the ranger's phone."

"No problem. Everything okay?"

"Uh, well *we're* all fine, but there might have to be a change of plans." I glanced up at the ranger, who was now busy scratching behind Hammy's soft ears. "There was a body in the woods. Someone died here last night. He was from the campsite right next to us." The ranger shook her head as if she still couldn't believe it.

"Oh no. That's terrible, Pepper. Was it an animal attack?"

I swallowed. "They think it's a possibility." *But they're wrong*, I said to myself.

42

Maggie exhaled. "So…?"

"Yep…"

"Darn."

Luckily my sister and I thought alike and didn't need full sentences, because I was spared from telling her not to come.

"I'm bummed, but you're absolutely right," Maggie said. "Are you guys leaving soon?"

Now it was my turn to exhale. "Yeah."

I could almost hear my sister's hand settle on her hip through the phone line. "Well that didn't sound very convincing. From the tone of your answer just a few moments ago, I can tell you don't think it was an animal." She whispered the next part, even though it was just us on the phone. "Pepper, you're not getting involved in this are you?"

"No, Mags. We're leaving. I promise." I swallowed.

Maggie sighed. "Okay, I'll see you soon. Call me when you get back."

"Will do. Kiss the kids for me. Sorry you have to break the news to them."

Snorting out a laugh, Maggie said, "Oh, they'll be fine. I'll take them to the lake tomorrow and they won't know the difference. I'm more worried about Josh and me, honestly. We really could've used a break from Pine Crest and Mom."

Letting out a groan, I repositioned the phone on my other ear. "Tell me about it."

Our mother's boyfriend of a year, Duncan, was moving into her house after living in an apartment surrounded by college kids for "much too long" in his opinion. I didn't mind Duncan. He was actually really nice and seemed just about smitten with our mother. But having another man move into the house we'd grown up in was going to be hard no matter what. Mom was making the process especially difficult, having finally decided to box up Dad's stuff, something she'd put off for years. Before I'd left for camping the other day, she'd called me seven times asking me when I was going to be able to look through the boxes of Dad's books to see what I wanted.

"You're actually kinda lucky you don't have any service," Maggie said. "If she didn't know where I lived, I would consider tossing my phone into the toilet to avoid her."

Laughing, I nodded. "It'll be over before we know it."

"I'm dreaming of that day," she said with a sigh. "Be safe, Peps."

"Love you, Mags."

I settled the phone back onto the cradle, feeling lighter already. Knowing my little niece and nephew were going to stay safe more than an hour away in Pine Crest made everything feel better. Especially since Maggie's insistence I not get involved had made my stomach flip with uncertainty. I definitely didn't want to stay another night, but could we really leave knowing the sheriff was possibly going to let a killer go?

"Here you go," the ranger said, handing Hammy back over the counter.

I took the dog with a feint smile. Setting Hammy down and hooking my hand through her leash, I thanked the woman and went back outside. Alex was still chatting with the ranger, but when I emerged, he waved goodbye and walked my way.

We walked in silence for a few moments before I couldn't keep quiet any longer. "So that's it. We can probably take off now, right?" I watched Alex out of the corner of my eye.

He nodded, staying frustratingly silent.

"You would really leave like this?" I asked, stopping. Hammy plopped her haunches down and looked up at me, like she was on my side.

"Peps, I don't like it either, but there's not a whole lot I can do if he's challenging my jurisdiction. He's right. This isn't my city; it's not even my county." Alex's eyes softened and he stepped closer to me, placing a hand on each of my shoulders. "We'll be able to do more from home anyway. I can fill my dad in on what we observed and see what information he can get about the case. As a detective, he has a whole lot more pull than a lowly officer. With his help, we should be able to dig up something." He finished with a wink.

I couldn't help but let my mouth quirk up into a grin. Leaning into him, I sighed. "Okay, okay. Let's go home."

Taking my hand, Alex led the way back to our camp. We passed by the college guys' camp on the way to ours. It was still quiet, but all of their stuff, their cars, their keg still sat in the site. About to pass by, my feet screeched to a halt when I caught sight of something in one of their car windows. Hammy anticipated my stop, and panted up at me as if asking, "what next?" but Alex kept walking. Still holding my hand, he jerked to a stop when he reached the end of my reach.

One glance at my face, and he didn't ask what was up, only followed my gaze to the white truck I was staring at. We walked forward. Stuck onto the back window of a white truck, in the bottom right corner, was the same star-like symbol I'd noticed stitched onto James's sweatshirt sleeve, next to the NWU marmot.

There may not be internet access up here, but I was starting to seriously wonder how I would even go about searching for the symbol once we got back home when I'd barely gotten a good look at it. I had been understandably focused on other things this morning, after all.

Always happy to smell something new, Hammy tugged me forward and began rooting around the tires, smelling wherever else the truck had been while Alex and I peered at the symbol.

Up this close and looking at this larger version, it became clear. It wasn't the top part of a star at all, but three capital As, positioned to look like the top three points of one.

I wrinkled my forehead in thought as I stared at the decal stuck to the mirrored surface of his tinted windows. Hadn't I seen it around campus? Was it the symbol for a club?

"Three As?" Alex said, squinting one eye.

"Isn't it a travel insurance company?" I asked.

"Not positioned like that."

I was about to check in the truck windows for anything else when I noticed Hammy had gotten herself all tangled up in her leash while we'd been inspecting the sticker. I bent to untangle her legs and was about to stand when something brown under the truck caught my eye. Well, everything was brown, actually, from the dried pine cones to the dust and the sticks, but there was a brown something which was quite a different texture than the forest debris surrounding it.

A brown leather journal.

"Hey, look at this," I said, reaching forward, I grabbed it, pulling it out into the light.

Alex frowned, but didn't say anything as I unwrapped the leather cord keeping it closed. When I opened the journal to the first page, I sucked in a surprised breath.

It looked like we weren't going to have to wait until we got access to the internet to find out the meaning of James's mysterious symbol.

6

"Well that's a surprise," Alex said as he read the first page of the journal over my shoulder. Forehead furrowed, he said, "Where did you find that exactly?" He knelt next to the truck, ducking to see underneath. "I'll need to show the sheriff when he comes back."

"Right here," I pointed, kneeling next to him. "It's gotta be James's, right? Maybe it fell out of his bag or something."

"Weird place for it to fall. Here, you said?" Alex looked at me until I nodded in confirmation. "It's really far under the tru…" his voice petered out as he seemed to stare at something on the ground. Edging in closer, Alex craned his neck to look up at the undercarriage of the truck. I could see his eyes narrow.

"What is it?" I asked.

Instead of answering, he pulled his phone out of his pocket. Turning on the flashlight, he aimed it under the truck, then back at the ground. Backing away, he turned the flashlight off and stood.

"The journal isn't wet, is it?" he asked.

I flipped it over. "Nope. Dry as a bone." I cringed slightly at my choice of words, but Alex didn't seem to care.

"The brake line has been cut on this truck." His forehead creased as he glanced down at the journal again.

Eyes wide, I gasped. "Seriously? Sheriff Langley will have to admit a mountain lion couldn't have done *that.*"

"Yeah." Alex scanned the campground. "Let's get back to our camp before Langley comes back."

Our friends were seated around the fire pit, perched on logs, chatting, and chomping on a late lunch of hot dogs and chili.

"Whatcha got there?" Liv asked when she looked up and noticed the journal clutched in my hand.

Before I could answer, Nate nonchalantly asked, "I didn't know there was a gift shop at the ranger's station. Did you purchase a diary, Pepper?"

"It's the dead guy's," I blurted out before anyone else could take a guess.

"You bought a dead man's journal at the gift shop?" Liv asked, squinting one eye.

Alex's face darkened. "She found it under that truck." He motioned to the white truck behind us now.

"You guys have to see this." I walked into the seating area around the fire pit and plopped down on the log. Hammy jumped up onto the log and Alex sat on my other side.

"Remember the symbol on the sleeve of his sweatshirt? Next to the NWU marmot?" I asked, flipping the journal open.

My friends nodded slowly.

"The thing that looked like a star?" Carson asked.

"Yes, but it's not a star. We walked up to one of their

cars because I spotted the same symbol. It's actually three As positioned like the west, north, and east of a compass rose." Opening the journal to the first page, I turned it around and showed them the large drawing of the symbol on the inside cover.

Liv tipped her head to one side. "What does it mean?"

"Alpha Alpha Alpha," I read from the next page. "Or TriAlphas."

Carson rubbed the back of his neck. "Like a fraternity?"

"I thought they went to NWU, though." Liv said. "We don't have a Greek system anymore."

The fact that NWU didn't allow sororities or fraternities anymore was a constant point of debate among student and faculty alike. They'd been disbanded over thirty years ago after there had been a series of student deaths linked to rush-specific hazing incidences. Some people loved the absence, seeing it as a pro when looking at NWU versus some of the other state colleges. Other people fought almost constantly to change the rule, to bring them back.

"Maybe we were wrong." Nate shrugged. "It's possible they don't go to NWU."

"And just happened to buy apparel from a small university they don't attend?" Victoria countered, surprising us all with another of her infrequent vocal opinions.

"Right," I said. "That seems oddly coincidental."

"Not to mention a huge waste of money," Liv added. "What?" she said when we all turned our attention on her. "Those sweatshirts aren't cheap."

Carson, who'd been sitting quietly, with ever-widening eyes, sucked in a quick breath.

"What is it, Moore?" Alex asked him.

"About three months ago, we got a new guy in student services. He came from the counseling offices and had all of these crazy stories about students coming in and spilling stuff to the people at the front desk before they even got in to see the counselor. Anyway, he was telling us about this student who was claiming mental and physical harm from a hazing which happened during rush week. When my coworker told him it wasn't possible, that fraternities were outlawed on our campus, he told him there was an underground frat still operating, and he was trying to expose them because of what they'd done to him. The kid said it had been around for something like thirty years. They thought the kid was just making it up, we all did, but now..." Carson shook his head.

"I've definitely seen this symbol before," I said, thinking back to where I might've come across it. The community message boards in the student center were full of club flyers, not to mention the various signs stapled onto telephone poles around campus touting tryouts and signups. "I never thought about it too hard, I guess. There are so many clubs to keep track of."

"An underground fraternity at Northern Washington University," Alex said, his exhale full of disbelief.

"And our neighbors are in it, deep," I told the others, turning the page to show them what Alex and I had already found. "Look." The next page was a list of the different officer positions in the frat, and who held each one.

The first line said, "President, James Mercer." It went on to list Matt Kincaid as the vice president, Kevin Thomas as the secretary, and Grady Gaines as the treasurer. There were other positions listed below, but I didn't recognize the other first names as any we'd heard from the group today.

Nate's forehead furrowed as he listened, and Liv blinked in disbelief.

"So our keg-stand crew is really a secret frat?"

"And someone killed their leader," Victoria said, startling us all with another sentence.

"What else is in there?" Carson asked, motioning to the journal.

I paged through it. "It goes on to describe the TriAlpha's mission statement, their vision and then it turns into more of a diary." From the snippets I read as I scanned it reminded me so much of the Thoreau I'd been reading lately. A lot of antiestablishment, live outside the norms. Though, instead of the peaceful tones of Walden, it definitely felt more on par with Thoreau's *Civil Disobedience*. I glanced up. "We think it has to be James's. Which means that must be his truck."

Everyone agreed except Alex, who I knew was not a fan of assumptions. Even so, he did give me a reluctant shrug; it was hard to deny.

"A truck on which the brakes appear to have been tampered with," Alex said.

The group gasped and started chatting about theories. I couldn't seem to focus on what they were saying, however; the journal was far too interesting. My fingers itched to page through it, read every entry—the journal was almost half full of entries.

"Should we call the sheriff? Let him know what we found?" I asked, turning to Alex.

"I'll call him," Alex said, putting a hand on my arm. "I'm going to the ranger's station to use their phone, so I'll be gone for about ten minutes." He held my gaze, then glanced down at the journal.

I squinted at him. When Alex raised his eyebrows and looked at my pocket, I began to understand his meaning. A smile curled across my face.

"Right. Good," I said. "We'll stay here."

He walked away, disappearing around a grouping of trees. Then I tied Hammy's leash to the nearest camp chair. Pulling my phone from my back pocket, I brought up the camera. As quickly as I could, I began snapping pictures of every page.

"Pepper, what in blazes are you…?" Nate sputtered.

I didn't have to answer him, because Liv shushed the man and said, "She's just making sure we have access to the evidence, too."

"If this sheriff is telling people it was a mountain lion, he's definitely not someone I trust," Carson added.

Nate's lips curved into a slow smile. "Ah, clever. Very clever, indeed. If that charlatan of a sheriff isn't going to properly investigate this murder, I wouldn't trust anyone else more than you and Alex to get to the bottom of it."

My heart swelled at Nate's vote of confidence. I instantly felt badly I'd ever thought he might actually hurt someone with the knife he'd brought.

"Thanks, guys," I said.

Victoria grinned; Carson and Liv nodded. I know Thoreau said he would rather sit alone on a pumpkin than crowded on a velvet cushion. But if these were the people with me, I'd happily sit anywhere with them.

"Hey, you'd better get going," Liv said, pointing to the journal.

She was right, Alex would be back soon. I resumed flipping and clicking. Flipping and clicking. My heart hammered from the adrenaline and the pace at which I worked, but by the time Alex came walking back into our camp, I'd just finished taking the photos. My fingers shook slightly as I wound the leather strap back around the journal. He gave me a wink, but other than that, pretended not to have any knowledge of what I'd done while he was gone.

The other conversations going on between my friends ceased, and I felt them lean toward Alex.

"He coming to pick it up?" I said, asking the question I assumed was on everyone's minds.

Alex nodded. "He was already on his way back. I talked with one of the deputies. Should be here—"

The sound of cars crunching to a stop behind us made us all stop.

"Now," Alex finished, taking in the two SUVs leaking college guys, a sheriff, and a deputy.

I stood and walked over to watch the guys. Some of their heads hung a little lower in sadness. A few of them kept checking over their shoulders, while others held their bodies tight and their faces even more so, exuding frustration. Maybe the questioning hadn't gone so well.

The sheriff pulled off his hat and scowled over at us. It was only then that I realized my friends had all stood and walked over next to me to watch as well.

"Well, I guess it's now or never," Alex said, pulling in a deep breath.

Placing the journal into his hands, I said, "Good luck" and leaned up to give him a kiss on the cheek.

The rest of us stayed behind as Alex walked over, journal in hand. Sheriff Langley raised his eyebrows, expression closed as he listened to Alex talk. He took the journal when Alex handed it to him, and I wrapped my fingers tightly around my phone. At least we had the pictures. After that, he followed Alex over to the white truck and they disappeared behind as Alex showed him where we'd found the journal as well as the brake fluid.

Unable to see them any longer, I turned back to our

camp. When I looked behind me, however, I gasped in terror. One of our camp chairs was… moving? It hobbled from one end of the fire pit to the other. My blood froze in my veins. Holy mother of… was our campsite haunted? Where ghosts real? Had James come back to tell us who'd really murdered him?

Upon hearing my surprise, my friends whirled around and caught sight of the possessed seat which seemed to be gaining speed. It skidded around Liv and Carson's tent, then headed straight for us. Just when I was about kick up some major dust and take off in the opposite direction, I caught sight of the black and white blur preceding the chair. Hammy's eyes were huge and rimmed in white as she locked them onto mine and headed my way.

I heard Carson let out a whoosh of air in what he'd never admit was relief.

"Oh, Ham!" I called, kneeling down to catch the flying mess of dog and leash and chair catapulting toward me.

Luckily, as Hammy crashed into my arms, Liv reached out and stopped the camp chair so it didn't come barreling into me, too. The little dog's body trembled as her legs continued to windmill, unsure if she was still being chased by the scary contraption.

"Shhh, shhh. Hammy, I'm so sorry, girl. I thought the chair would be heavy enough to keep you in one place," I cooed into her ear as I smoothed the hair on her back and scratched behind her ear.

After a few seconds of that, she was still panting, but had calmed considerably. I undid her leash, so she was no longer attached to the evil chair, and everyone helped me in showering her with praise and scratches.

By the time she was back to normal, Alex was walking back toward us. We all checked behind him to see the sheriff walk over to the frat guys who were now sitting around their own campfire. After talking with them for a minute and collecting a few things I couldn't quite identify into evidence bags, he and his deputy came our way.

"Evening," the sheriff said, tipping his hat. "I'm going to need to take a look at any knives you folks have with you."

7

My shock at the sheriff asking for anything we had which could've been used as the murder weapon was quickly eclipsed by my excitement that he actually seemed to be taking this murder seriously. *Good find, Alex,* I thought. It seemed the brake-line clue had set some kind of fire under the reluctant sheriff.

"I have a pocket knife," Alex said, standing and moving toward his truck, where our packed bags sat.

I shook my head, but Liv got up and went over to the cooking utensils she'd brought, among which was a small knife.

Carson put his hands up. "You interested in a pair of old scissors? Because that's all I've got in my car."

Sheriff Langley nodded seriously. Carson's smile faded and he moved to get them out of his car. Then everyone looked to Nate and Victoria. I held my breath, remembering the scary switchblade.

Victoria swiveled her head to look at Nate.

He stood up. "Oh, fine. But for the record, I think it's ludicrous." He walked over to his bag and rummaged in it until he pulled out the large knife. "If I wanted to kill someone, it would be much easier to poison them than slit their throat." Nate wrinkled his nose. "So messy." He held out the knife, dropping it into the bag the deputy had opened.

Pressing my lips together, I tried to hold back the groan clawing at my throat. *Naaaaate*, my thoughts whined. Could the man make it through any situation without making a complete creep of himself?

Both the sheriff and the deputy stared at Nate wide-eyed, telling me I wasn't alone in my wonderings about his words.

"He doesn't—" I stuttered.

"He wouldn't—" Liv added.

"We've all been drinking his coffee and none of us are dead." Everyone's attention turned to Victoria who just shrugged at her matter-of-fact point.

"I want that back," Nate said, pointing at the knife before he turned and walked back to his seat near Victoria. "It's my favorite knife."

Liv closed her eyes to hide an eye roll. The man could not be helped. Seriously, though. Who has a *favorite* knife? Serial murderers, that's who. And Nate, apparently.

The sheriff and his deputy said they'd be in touch. They turned to leave, each climbing into a now-empty SUV.

Switching my attention back to the frat guys, I noticed they began passing around a large bottle once the officers left. It was dark amber and appeared to burn on the way down—if their scrunched faces were any indication.

"To James," we heard them say dejectedly, holding their disposable cups up in the air.

My heart ached. They were having a little wake for their friend. The whole situation was made even worse thinking about the killer possibly sitting among them—one of their friends.

"I think maybe we should go," I whispered. We had all the clues we were going to get, hanging around here, plus these guys deserved a little privacy.

Alex nodded and the rest of our group agreed. Just as we began to move toward our tents, we heard Kevin bellow out, "Hey coffee guy, the sheriff said he has more questions, and we have to wait until he comes back, so we're drinking. Join us for a drink in James's honor. Bring your frien —oomf!"

Kevin doubled over as Matt punched him in the stomach. "Dude, shut up." A few other guys whispered admonishments at Kevin.

Alex's mouth had already begun shaping the beginning of a "no." But when he saw Matt wanted to keep us away, he pressed his lips together and looked to Nate.

"I'm not going to have any, neither should anyone who's driving, but that doesn't mean passengers can't," he said, ignoring how the other guys definitely didn't seem to want us to come over.

Nate pulled in a deep breath, seemingly surprised to be the one on which our invitation hinged. After a second, he said, "Let's go."

I eyed Alex as we followed after Nate.

"What're you up to?" I whispered.

"Thoreau said water is the only drink for a wise man," Alex quoted, arching one eyebrow.

"Yeah?" I said.

"I'm counting on it being true." He winked at me and walked into their camp.

I smiled, understanding clearly. Pulling Hammy closer, I whispered, "Let's go get some questions answered, girl."

WE SCHLEPPED ourselves back to our campsite a couple hours later, when the sun was beginning to dip beneath the jagged horizon of pine trees and mountain tops. Defeat hung off our bodies, pulling us down like the heaviest backpacks.

After all of that time we'd learned zero information about James or the TriAlphas. Zero.

Each time we tried to bring up James, the guys would just yell out his name, raise their cups, drink, and then start talking about a never-ending list of sports teams. This was either the dumbest group of men I'd ever encountered, or the most clever.

Eventually, we had to stop mentioning James because they were becoming too inebriated with all of the random cheers forcing them to drink. And unlike some people— ahem, Liv and myself—whose inhibitions fall considerably in correlation to their level of intoxication, these guys seemed to become less and less likely to share information the more they drank.

"I can't believe they're still standing," Carson yawned and rubbed the back of his hand against his eyes. He leaned into Liv, who guided him to their tent and began pulling up the stakes.

Alex shook his head. By the way he'd let out a few exas- perated sighs, I could tell he shared my disappointment at our inability to find out anything. He began to perform the same task with our tent. I moved to help him.

Once everyone had loaded their tents and bags, we stood there, everyone looking around uneasily.

"So…" Liv said, cringing as the sun dipped down behind the mountains. "I guess we'll see you back in town."

There was a whole slew of unspoken statements clinging to my friend's words. The most obvious being: this is weird, and awkward, and no one wants to be the first to peel out of this campground and away from all of the terrible things which had happened here.

Even though no one spoke these thoughts, I was almost positive it was what was on all our minds as we looked reluctantly around our camp. We'd all driven separately, a couple in each car, so because we were splitting up, it almost felt as if we needed some sort of conclusion, closure with this place.

"Well, that was… fun," Victoria said, her tone speaking to the awkwardness evident in each of our stances.

"I personally could've done without the dead body," Carson said, shrugging.

We all laughed. And agreed. Then waved and got into our respective vehicles. Once I was buckled in, I sighed. Thoreau had lasted two years, two months, and two days out in the woods by Walden Pond. I couldn't even make it the two days.

Depressing or not, soon we were bumping along an unpaved back highway, Hammy jumping between the two of us from window to window. I pulled out my phone and pulled up the pictures of the journal.

Alex's chest rose and fell in a deep breath.

"Hey," I said, watching the forest thin as we neared civilization once more. "I was disappointed we didn't learn anything from them, too. But now that I'm thinking about it, I can't believe we thought we could just waltz over there, expecting them to spill every secret about their underground fraternity."

Alex nodded.

"They've kept it a secret from the university and the

town of Pine Crest for decades, it sounds," I added. "That takes skill and commitment. I'm definitely guilty of underestimating these guys, too, and it almost makes me wonder if they act like partiers, so no one would think of accusing them of hiding such a big secret."

"Well, we tried, at least," he said. "Read me some of this journal. If they won't spill about what happened, maybe James will."

Flipping past the first few pictures, containing the pages that held the names of the fraternity leaders and their symbol, I stopped on a page holding the frat's motto. "Disobedience is the true foundation of liberty—Henry David Thoreau," I read.

I sucked in a quick breath. Sure I'd recognized some of the same antiestablishment-type rhetoric when scanning through the pages earlier, but the fraternity's motto was actually a quote from *Civil Disobedience?*

Alex snorted. "I'm sorry. I know your dad really liked the guy, but that quote couldn't be further from the truth. Disobedience isn't the foundation of liberty—honor and loyalty are."

Patting his arm, I realized I wasn't one hundred percent sure what was, but now was not the time to get into a debate about something like this. I focused on searching through the other pictures. "It's not really a journal, per se. There aren't entries by date. Instead, it seems to be some sort of handbook about the frat." I kept scanning. "I mean, he's got a list of current members, the ways in which the members are expected to support each other, and even an in-depth analysis of the frats weak spots."

"Any list of who might've killed him in there?" Alex laughed.

I stared at my phone, zooming in on certain entries too

small for me to read. I zeroed in on an entry titled, "Internal and External Cracks" as Hammy jumped from Alex's lap over to mine.

"Uh, maybe…" I whispered, my eye moving over the page which held a list of what seemed to be something one could use as blackmail for each person. Everybody but James. "Listen to this," I said to Alex. "He wrote here that Matt wanted to take over as president; Kevin and James were fighting over the same girl, and Grady was fighting with James over something to do with the house they're all living in together. Gosh, I'm surprised a guy as paranoid as James didn't keep a mirror with him at all times just to watch his back. He seriously seems to have thought through every possible thing which could take down him and the fraternity."

"Maybe he was spending so much time watching his back he didn't notice what was right in front of him." Eyebrows raising, Alex kept his attention on the road as he brought up James's unfortunate end. "Any of those disagreements sound like good motives?"

I bit my lip. "Maybe. Apparently it was well known within the fraternity Matt wanted to take over as president *and* he and James just happened to get into a physical fight the night James was killed." My tone was thoughtful as I let the statement hang in the quiet of the truck cab as the tires transitioned onto paved roadway. Hammy began to circle on the seat, finally curling up into a ball next to my thigh and letting out a huge sigh.

"Vice president to president doesn't seem like a overly huge jump in power. I mean, I don't know anything about the structure of their fraternity, but it doesn't seem like enough to kill over." Alex shook his head.

I agreed. "There must be something more, something

worth fighting over." Unsure what that was, however, I moved onto the next thing James had identified as an internal problem. I said, "Get this. Kevin and James were fighting over a girl. Kevin brought a girl he'd been seeing to one of their parties and she ended up staying the night… with James." Scrunching up my shoulders, I said, "A jerk move, but also not something worth killing over."

"That hasn't stopped people in the past. Depends on how he felt about this girl. Or if this was an isolated incident. This could be something James did a lot."

"True." I smiled as Hammy began to snore. "And then there's Grady's dad owning the house they've been staying at. He doesn't mention where this house is, though." I squinted one eye as I tried to picture where a secret frat house could be hiding my hometown. "We definitely need more information about each of these disputes. Right now, there's not enough to go on. Plus, there are three more written here involving people whose names I don't recognize." I scooted the document around on my screen so I could read the whole thing. "I mean, here's a disagreement with someone named Chloe and even an issue with one of the deans at the university." I shook my head.

"Sounds like we've got some reading to do," Alex said, glancing at my phone.

"Yup." Settling my hand onto Hammy's back, I scrunched my fingers down into the fur by her neck.

8

The next morning, Liv was already awake when Hammy and I stumbled out of my room around eight. Liv was an early riser by nature, but I figured she might need a little more sleep after our restless night of camping. While I wasn't necessarily surprised to see Liv up this early, she was definitely surprised to see me.

Her eyes widened, and she checked the teal clock hanging on the wall next to the door. "Whoa. Did you forget you're still technically on vacation?" she asked.

I groaned. "I couldn't sleep anymore. My mind got working on this case. I can't seem to shut it off. Figured I'd just get up and get started doing some research. Alex said he was going to run everything by his dad last night and see if he could help out, so I'm going to head over there."

She grinned. "Look at you and the detective, getting along."

Alex's father, Detective Valdez, and I hadn't necessarily gotten off on the best foot a couple years ago when he'd first taken over at the station. Then again, Alex and I hadn't started out smoothly either, and now I couldn't seem to picture my life without him.

"Well, I don't know if the detective expected me to join this morning, so I'm not sure 'getting along' is the right way to describe what's about to happen."

Snorting, Liv said, "By now, he should expect you to show up anytime there's a case to be solved."

After walking Hammy and getting myself ready, I started out toward the Valdez residence. Their house was about a twenty-minute walk away, but I could cut a good five minutes off if I took a shortcut through the edge of campus closest to our apartment.

Fifteen minutes later, Hammy and I were slipping through their front gate and trotting up the small garden path to the gray house with white trim. From the manicured garden to the clean interior of the house, Alex and his father were just as meticulous in their domestic pursuits as they were in their investigative ones. I rapped my knuckles on the front door and waited. Hammy tugged on the leash when Alex opened the door a few moments later, pulling on a heather-gray T-shirt.

"Morning," Alex smiled. Between the rumpled look of his hair and the glimpse of his abs I'd just gotten, I almost forgot why I came over.

"Hey." I walked inside, those dark-brown eyes acting like tractor beams pulling me forward.

Alex leaned down and kissed me as he closed the door behind us, making me wonder if the case couldn't wait for just a *little* bit. I closed my eyes and leaned into him. His arm snaked around my waist and he tugged me close. He smelled like minty toothpaste and soap and I wanted to breathe him in.

"Miss Brooks," I heard from somewhere beyond Alex's

lips. Detective Valdez cleared his throat as I opened my eyes, heat burning up my neck and into my cheeks.

"Morning, Detective." Even after knowing him for a couple years—over a year of which he'd been my boyfriend's father—I still couldn't manage to call the man anything other than Detective Valdez. I pulled away from Alex and gave his father a quick salute.

Normally I really didn't mind that Alex still lived with his father. He may have been twenty-four and in a career which paid him more than enough to afford his own place, but I knew he and his dad were still getting over the loss of Alex's mom two years ago. She'd been a police officer as well, down where they'd lived in California, and had been shot in the line of duty. They'd moved up here to start over in a quiet town that didn't hold so many tough memories. So the two of them still living together, I totally got. It was just in times like these when I found his paternal presence a little less than endearing.

Alex didn't seem to mind that his dad was standing right in front of us, however, pulling me against him as I pivoted to face the detective. His closeness and his dad's presence flustered me a bit and I tried to step away, but ended up getting myself completely wrapped in Hammy's leash from all of my turning.

Taking Hammy's leash from my hand, Alex helped unwind me.

"Come in the kitchen, you two. I'll make you something to eat for breakfast," Detective Valdez said, cracking a quick smirk as I untangled myself from Hammy. Normally, the man wore a serious expression as religiously as I wore leggings as if they were real pants.

After unclipping Hammy, Alex moved to hang her leash on the coat rack as his father disappeared down the hall.

Biting my lip, I looked back at Alex who nodded encouragingly. He knew I was still slightly intimidated by his dad, just like he was around my mom. But the only way to get over that was to get to know him, right? After a deep breath, I followed Alex and Hammy into the kitchen.

Alex perched on a stool next to an eating bar running along the outer edge of a peninsula countertop, so I sat on the one next to him.

"So I hear you two had quite the run-in with Jeremiah Langley yesterday," the detective said as he pulled out a bag of pancake mix. He grabbed a skillet, then set it on the stove, turning on a burner to let it warm up.

"You could say that." At the promise of food, my stomach grumbled greedily.

Turning toward me, Alex said, "Dad's had to work with him a few times and apparently he's always a little closed off."

"That's definitely putting it diplomatically," Detective Valdez said with a chuckle.

The laugh surprised me, but not as much as his candor. I hadn't ever known Alex's father to put anything any other way than 'diplomatically.' Maybe the guy was actually starting to loosen up around me, dare I say, trust me? I felt my shoulders relax a little.

"You didn't hear this from me, but he's not exactly well liked around here."

"Now *that's* putting it diplomatically," Alex said, repeating his dad from a second ago. "I was just about at the point where I was wondering if we were dealing with a *Jaws* situation."

Detective Valdez raised his eyebrows, as if it made sense to him.

I glanced between them. "What does a shark have to do with this?"

"The sheriff in *Jaws* tries to keep the deaths quiet so it doesn't ruin the busy, tourism season for the town," Alex said.

"Oh." I nodded. "He didn't want it to get out and ruin the last big camping weekend of the summer."

"Well, that's unavoidable at this point," the detective said. "I was just on the phone with him earlier this morning. They've officially declared it a murder. He sent the boys home this morning, but only because he didn't have enough evidence to hold them any longer. He wanted me to keep an eye on them."

I almost fell off my stool, but the detective reached for a bowl and began measuring ingredients into it, as if he discussed police matters with me all the time.

"So he's calling it a murder now?" I asked, tripping over the words in my surprise.

Detective Valdez nodded slowly. "Yeah, the medical examiner just confirmed the victim died from a nonserrated blade cut to the throat. Based on the cut, the killer was a few inches shorter than the victim. They also found traces of polyglycol ether in the wound, which is a solvent used in brake fluid, which means the same knife was used to cut the brakes as kill the victim. But you didn't hear that from me, either." He winked at me then turned to whisk the ingredients together in his bowl.

Blinking, I looked over at Alex, who was smiling at me. Honestly, I wasn't sure how he *wasn't* freaking out. His dad trusted me. Me!

The sizzle of the pancakes as they hit the skillet must've been some sort of signal for Alex, because he stood and began putting plates and silverware on the table behind us.

"You want some coffee?" Alex asked me, pulling a few mugs from the cupboard.

I scoffed. "Always." Then, after eyeing the pot of black coffee sitting in the coffeemaker, I asked, "Do you have any creamer?"

"None of that fancy stuff you like." Alex shook his head. "Dad's a coffee snob like you, though, so he only buys the best. You should try it without all of the sugar and syrups you and Liv pile into your cups."

Glancing over at the detective, I sighed. "Sure. Why not."

Did I want to drink black coffee? Not especially. But I'd also just gotten a hint of what it was like to have the detective's approval, and I was hungry for more. Smiling, Alex poured me a cup.

Minutes later, we sat down at the table and Detective Valdez walked over with a plate of steaming pancakes. He flipped two of them onto my plate, causing my breath to catch in my throat. He'd made them in the shape of a P and a B for my initials. Just like my dad used to do.

"Thank you," I stuttered out the words, caught off guard by the sweet gesture.

He blinked and dipped his chin, moving over to Alex, who got an A and a Mickey Mouse head. Alex chuckled and shook his head, but reached for the syrup nonetheless. "Thanks, Dad."

And then it hit me. Detective Valdez was just that, a dad. Alex's dad. And maybe, after close to two years, he was starting to trust me just like Dad would've done with Alex— wary at first, but once he saw how much he cared for me, he would've let up.

My heart ached at the reminder Alex would never get to meet my dad. I think they would've liked each other. To take my mind off the sadness building in my chest, I took my first sip of the jet-black coffee sitting in front of me.

Eyes wide, I smacked my tongue. "Oh, that's not half bad."

Detective Valdez smirked, sending a wink my way before he started cutting up his pancakes. "So tell me," he said without looking up. "These guys are coming back to town. Do I have any murderers on my hands here?"

Alex and I glanced at each other for a moment, but then I started filling him in on what we'd learned so far.

———

AN HOUR LATER, stomachs full of pancakes, Alex and I walked, hand in hand, along the quiet walkways of the university campus. Hammy sniffed happily along the edge of the concrete footpath while we reveled in the last few days of real quiet on the campus.

Classes would begin this week, but for now the place was pretty deserted; only students who'd stayed for summer quarter or were moving in the dorms extra early were joining us in the late summer sunshine. Alex's dad had to go into the station to check in on a few cases he was working on, and we'd decided to take a little walk to soak in some of the beautiful day.

The cornflower-blue sky was vast and just about cloudless, if you didn't count one or two tiny puffs hanging out near the peaks of the nearby mountain range. The campus grass had just recently been cut in preparation for the new quarter. The smell of warm earth surrounded us like a toddler's security blanket.

"Beats California, huh?" I said, shooting a playful smirk at Alex.

He tsked and bumped my shoulder with his. "I don't know. There's not much that can beat a true Santa Cruz sunset." His eyes narrowed as if he were seeing it in his mind's eye. Then he turned toward me and winked. "Besides your smile, of course."

I snuggled closer to him as we continued to walk. There were many times I wondered if he and his father would ever want to move back to California. As much as I wished him enough closure about his mother's death, that he wouldn't look like someone had sucker punched him in the gut every time he thought of her, I also secretly hoped he would never forgive California enough to move back.

Walking over the stone bridge arching over Campus Creek, we took a sharp right and headed down a small hill down toward the bank. Next to a beautiful willow tree was a bench. Ever since I'd been a kid, walking through campus with only dreams of attending the local university, it had been one of my favorite places to come and read or think.

Alex and I sat, Hammy jumped in between us, settling on Alex's lap, her tongue lolling out of her mouth as she dog-smiled up at him. I would've been slightly jealous if I didn't completely share in her infatuation.

"Remember when we both ended up here one evening after we first met?" Alex said, pulling in a deep breath of the cool breeze kicking up off the creek.

I scoffed. "Uh, yeah. I thought you completely hated me and then the next second I thought you were going to kiss me, but you really were just leaning forward to pick a leaf out of my hair."

Alex chuckled. "I was totally going to kiss you, but I thought *you* hated me and I chickened out. That leaf wasn't even in your hair. I picked it up off the bench and just pretended it was why I was leaning in."

I smiled at the memory. My attraction to Alex after he started working in the library had been hard to deny, even when he'd been mostly mad at me for trying to get involved with his dad's murder investigation. That day on this bench had been one of the first times I'd actually thought he might not despise me as much as he pretended to up until that point.

As if to prove how much things had changed since then, Alex leaned over and kissed me.

"And here we are again," I said after his lips left mine. "Dealing with another dead body."

"Some things never change."

Campus Creek trickled happily by, setting the perfect relaxing background music.

"What else did you find out from your reading last night?" Alex asked after a few silent moments, calling to mind the reason I must've woken early with the case on my mind: I'd gone to bed reading all about the drama between the TriAlpha members.

"Like I told your dad, the frat seems to be completely Thoreau-crazy." I thought back to the many tirades James went on about in the journal regarding the "establishment." The journal had gone into great detail about the fight the founding members had gone through with the university decades earlier when they'd banned the Greek system on campus.

"If I don't have to hear anything more about Thoreau ever again, it'll be too soon."

"Well, the TriAlphas definitely seem to support more of the *Civil Disobedience* ideals from Thoreau, not as much the environment-loving transcendentalist we see through the pages of *Walden*."

"There didn't seem to be a difference to me," Alex snorted.

I tipped my head in concession. He had a point. Though there was a lot about the beauty of nature within the *Walden* ideals, there was still quite a lot about shirking the status quo. "Thoreau certainly knew what he believed, and so does this secret frat." When Alex raised his eyebrows in question, I added, "They believe the university banning fraternities was the best thing that could've happened, because now they didn't have to play by its overbearing rules. Without regulation, they could finally take care of their own, that secrecy allowed them to do even more for their members than they were able to as a university supervised entity."

Alex cleared his throat, in full police officer mode now. "I don't know. Rarely are the things people do in the shadows, outside of the law, good."

"Right? Reminded me a little of *The Godfather* as I was reading. Everything's corrupt, but at least we can win at the corruption game."

"I think you're giving them a little too much credit there. The mob is pretty complex. These guys are supposed to be running a secret fraternity, yet their president wrote everything down in a journal."

I continued. "That's part of it, I think. They want to seem like stupid meatheads. It makes it much more difficult to believe they took out James on purpose."

"*If* they did," Alex said, reminding me nothing was for sure. "His brakes having been cut shows that someone was trying to get rid of James any way they could."

Widening my eyes, I said, "Oh, you have no idea."

Intrigued, Alex leaned in.

"Tell me, what's the most important thing to a fraternity, especially one like this?" I asked.

"Loyalty? Tradition?" Alex guessed.

I touched my pointer finger to my nose. "And so James's plans to move the frat to SWU and take it public would've been a pretty big problem to the TriAlphas. Worth killing him over."

9

Alex's eyebrows rose at the implications of the information I'd just shared with him. The wind picked up and rushed through the long, lazy branches of the willow tree to our left. I took a moment to take a deep breath of the fresh breeze.

I knew I needed to consider suspects outside of the fraternity, but if the guys knew of James's plans to uproot an organization that'd been in one place for decades, it was a pretty good motive for murder, and one only the members of the fraternity would've cared about. It was something I hadn't shared with Detective Valdez earlier, wanting to get a little more information before I decided what it meant.

Not to be outdone, Alex said, "I may not have found something as good, but I still think we need to add a few names to this suspect list." He pulled out his phone and started typing something into a browser. "When I searched for TriAlphas or even their symbol, all I could find was from when they were a fraternity here thirty years ago, nothing new. But when I looked up secret fraternity at NWU, I got a hit."

Intrigued, I leaned closer to Alex on the bench to see what he found. While my job had been to read through as much of the journal pictures as I could last night—I'd gotten through a good half of them before I'd fallen asleep, thank you very much—Alex's job had been to see if the internet held any more information than we'd gotten in the journal.

Alex pulled his phone away for a moment, meeting my gaze with his. "I know *The Frond* isn't necessarily your favorite…"

I scoffed. Okay, that might be the understatement of the year. *The Frond* was the university's unofficial periodical, the tongue-and-cheek alternative to the serious *Campus Chronicle*. I'd been happy to laugh at their silly stories and often undocumented sources with everyone else on campus until they'd pointed the finger at my favorite professor a couple years ago as the most likely suspect in an ongoing murder investigation. Since then, I'd held a huge grudge against the organization.

Ignoring my unapologetic feelings, Alex continued. "But, if it's any consolation, she only *used* to work there, probably hates them too. Get this, her name is Chloe," Alex said.

Eyes wide, I asked, "Chloe, as in one of the cracks?" My nose wrinkled at my word choice. "I mean, you know… the journal. James's 'Internal and External Cracks.'"

Alex laughed. "I think so. Chloe French used to write for *The Frond*, but before summer break she wrote a story on a secret fraternity, thinking her editor would be pleasantly surprised by her initiative and the inside scoop she'd gotten. But when she brought the finished story to them, her editor wouldn't publish it no matter what. She eventually ended up publishing the content on a blog of hers in the wake of her frustration with the paper."

"I can't imagine they liked that." I cringed.

"They didn't. Fired her and refused to give her a reference for other papers. But that wasn't even the worst of it. Within hours of her publishing the story, Chloe started getting anonymous warnings to take it down. When she didn't take them seriously, they morphed into death threats, she says."

"She says?"

"There isn't any actual proof of these threats anymore. She's been documenting everything on her blog. When she took her computer in to show one of the deans and campus security, they told her they didn't see what she was talking about. She took her laptop back and the threats were gone."

"Erased?" I asked.

"Or they never existed in the first place and she's crazy. It's what she claims, at least. Since then, the problems have been less direct. Her name is mud; she hasn't been able to get a job at any other paper within twenty-five miles, and when she even looked into moving to another university, they told her some of her writing credits wouldn't transfer."

I shivered, the welcome breeze from minutes ago now feeling like an eerie chill with this new information.

"This feels like a movie or something. Either the girl is crazy or someone is working very hard to make it appear that she is."

"Not just someone." Alex arched an eyebrow. "There are at least twenty calling her out as a liar and a lunatic."

Pulling up the pictures of James's journal on my phone and holding it in front of him, I asked, "Switch? I know you want to get into these, and I need to read whatever got this Chloe chick death threats."

Swapping phones with me, Alex was immediately absorbed into the world of the TriAlphas and James's intense paranoia about everyone and everything threatening his precious fraternity. I focused on Chloe's story. The title read, "Fraternizing with Fear." I began reading, stopping to snort at her commentary on how Pine Crest was a nice town, but the locals were a little intense, when she was setting the scene for her story. I heard Alex exhale in disbelief at something in James's journal at the same moment. Regardless of my disagreement with her statement, I dove back in. The peaceful sounds of Campus Creek in the background felt so oddly matched with the dark material I found in the article.

Chloe went on and on about odd happenings on campus, people getting grades they didn't seem to deserve, disciplinary action which simply disappeared, and a few other things which were probably pure coincidence. Honestly, this whole thing sounded a lot like a gossip column. But I knew Alex wouldn't have taken it seriously without good reason, so there had to be something in here that had caught his eye. I kept reading and I found it.

I was alerted to the existence of this fraternity when Dylan Oakes, a student here at NWU and a member of the varsity baseball team came to me, hoping I'd help tell his story. You see, he'd participated in the spring "rush" in an attempt to gain acceptance into the fraternity. "It was terrible," Dylan told me. "They locked us in a basement for hours without food or water. When they finally let us out—they made us play a trivia game and each time we got something wrong, we had to take a shot. Apparently, I passed out. Another pledge had taken me to the hospital when I wouldn't wake up. My blood-alcohol level was almost four times the legal limit," Dylan recounted when I interviewed him, only weeks after his accident. "If he hadn't brought me in, I would've died. As it was, it took me two days to recover."

When Dylan made it out of the hospital, the members of the fraternity found him and told him that he was never to talk about what happened or they would ruin his life. He was denied acceptance, as was the pledge who saved him. Dylan didn't listen, however, telling everyone from the school counselors to the dean of students. But after news of a failed routine sports drug test surfaced from weeks earlier, Dylan's account was quickly thrown out as an attempt to save his scholarship and spot on the team. "I've never done drugs in my life," Dylan assured me. "And I definitely didn't fail any of my tests. They planted it to discredit my story. I was kicked off the team and I lost my scholarship."

One has to wonder if the mysterious death of Ethan Emsworth three years ago has anything to do with the existence of this secret fraternity. If so, Dylan's story could be only one of many, but the others are too scared to speak up, like the pledge who saved Dylan's life. He has remained silent and has refused any attempts I've made to contact him.

It is because of this danger that I don't name the fraternity here. I believe they've killed before and wouldn't be above killing again. As it is, I think I'm putting myself in grave danger by posting even this.

I let out a long breath as I finished reading. A quick scan of her other posts seemed to confirm what Alex had told me about her mental stability being called into question after the "threats" she received turned out to be nonexistent.

Indecision made me chew on my bottom lip while I thought. On one hand, I could see where her editor was coming from. The piece was full of wild speculations, unsubstantiated conjectures, and only one discredited witness. If I hadn't spent the last twenty-four hours completely consumed with James's death, finding his journal, and trying to get information out of his campmates, I probably would've written her off as certifiable, too.

But between the tight-lipped keg-stand crew, the mysterious journal, and the cut brake line on James's truck, I was beginning to see some glimmers of truth within the madness.

Alex, sensing I'd finished, glanced up from my phone. There were far more journal entries than there were of Chloe's blog posts.

"So?" he asked.

I shared with him my observations and my hesitations, ending with, "We definitely need to add both Chloe and Dylan to our suspect list. If what she says is true, either of them would have motive to get revenge on the frat, or James in particular, being the president."

Alex—ever-rational—said, "*If* what she says is true, you're right. Her later posts have a very manic feel to them and that doesn't quite sit right with me."

"Yeah, I'm worried it could be a case of the hound, bay horse, and turtledove."

Squeezing his eyes shut, Alex rubbed them with the heels of his palms. "That sounds vaguely familiar. Why do I have a terrible feeling it has to do with Thoreau?"

Ignoring him, I continued. "In *Walden*, Thoreau mentions how he lost his hound, bay horse, and turtledove. When he describes them to the locals, some say they've heard the hound baying or the distant clomp of the horse's hooves. Some people even mention having seen the dove fly away, disappearing behind a cloud. Thoreau mentions these people often spend the rest of their lives searching for his lost animals, growing to care about them as if they'd been the ones to lose them. There's a large group of scholars who believe the animals never existed, they were merely analogies for friendship, passion, and escape. They believe the people Thoreau asked to help only took up his search because they too were looking for those same amorphous ideals, not physical animals."

Alex blinked, obviously running on too little sleep to dive into literary analysis with me this early.

"What if Chloe heard Dylan's fabricated story and turned it into her own? She's obviously holding on to issues where the university is concerned, expressing angst over people passing classes they didn't attend and others getting away with illegal activities. What if Dylan's story about the frat spoke to an ideal she was already searching for?"

Alex glanced down at Hammy, curled up in between us, scratching behind her ears as he pondered my words. "Okay, but what if Thoreau actually did lose those animals? The guy didn't seem to be particularly with it, to me."

I chuckled, but let Alex continue.

"What if Chloe had, in fact, seen the dove, heard the hound and the horse, but didn't know they were important until Dylan came along and made her aware? Our brain doesn't like to be confused, so when something unaccountable happens, it will latch onto the easiest explanation we're given. Especially if there's a group of people feeding us these easy stories, bent on the general public not asking questions, not looking deeper. A person can see something, but not know its importance until someone else gives it a name or a purpose."

My mouth dropped open as I listened, lips finally quirking up into a smile as he finished. Okay, maybe he was ready for literary analysis. "Have I told you lately that I absolutely love you?" I said, leaning over to kiss him.

"Not nearly enough," he said with a wink.

"So," I said through a long exhale. "We need to figure out if Chloe is chasing real animals or the idea of animals."

"Sure," Alex said. "We now know there is a secret frat on campus, so that's one point in her court."

"And James was worried enough about her to write

about her in the journal. She's sounding more and more credible by the second. She still goes to NWU, then?" I asked, not having missed the fact that she'd been trying to transfer elsewhere.

"I think so," Alex said. "Based on what I could glean from her blog."

"Well we've got to meet with this girl, then." I opened up a new email under her "Contact Me" section and began to type in my information and then my message.

Chloe, My name is Pepper Brooks. I just read your article. I believe you and I want to talk. Can we meet? I own Brooks' Books in town if you feel more comfortable talking in person instead of responding through your site. Hope to hear from you soon.

I passed the phone to Alex, letting him read what I'd written.

"Good call acknowledging her fears so you're already on her side." He read through the rest and handed the phone back to me.

Satisfied, I sent my message. "And now we wait." I sighed, blinking up happily at the sun as its rays blanketed my face.

I knew we were still investigating a murder and there was a killer out there, but it felt so different being back home. It felt safer than the quiet woods, ironically more peaceful when we didn't have to look over our shoulders every other moment, worried there might be a killer searching for another unsuspecting throat.

And it wasn't just the killer we had to worry about, either. Fueled by the stories and the journal, this fraternity was growing into a looming presence in my mind. An evil power bent on quieting anyone who threatened its anonymity. If Chloe and Dylan were to be believed, the TriAlphas had the means and connections to ruin lives.

I sighed. Even surrounded by clues in this ever-deepening conundrum of a case, I was back in Pine Crest, sitting in one of my favorite spots on campus, curled up next to Alex and Hammy.

The buzzing of my phone in my pocket cut through the peaceful silence a few minutes later, making me jump. Alex moved his arm so I could sit up straight and pull the phone out of my pocket. Hammy snorted in surprise, the movement waking her up from the nap she was taking, nestled in between us. I groaned as I noticed the call was from my mother.

10

Finger hovering over my phone screen, I considered not answering. I didn't particularly want to break the lovely, quiet scene of the creekside bench and willow tree. But I also knew my mother and her penchant for being persistent. If I didn't answer now, she would only call back in a few minutes. Holding my breath, I pressed the answer button.

"Hey, Mom," I said, cringing at what I knew what was coming.

"Honey, hi! I hear you had to cut your trip short. That's terrible."

I nodded. "Yeah, especially for the dead guy."

Seeing I wasn't going anywhere, Hammy settled her chin back on my thigh as Alex scratched behind her ear.

Mom tsked at my comment. I could tell she was pacing by the clicking sound of her heels in the background. Heels meant she was at work, on a Sunday. The woman had a problem.

Confirming my suspicions, she said, "I'm at the office, but I'm just about to head home and since you're back early,

I was wondering if you wouldn't mind stopping by and looking through those boxes of your dad's books I set aside for you."

Taking a minute to breathe and temper my tone, I said, "Sure. We could do that." I glanced over at Alex and he raised his eyebrows, aware I'd just volunteered him to come with me.

"We? Oh, is Alex with you? It would be wonderful to see him!" she said, loud enough for Alex to hear.

He smiled. My super-scary lawyer mother had practically waterboard-level interrogated the guy the first time she'd met him. After that, it had taken her a while to warm up to him after he'd arrested her new boyfriend, Duncan, in a murder case. But ever since he'd saved my life after I'd been kidnapped last year, the guy could do no wrong in my mother's eyes. She adored him, in fact.

"Yep, he's here," I said. "We'll be over in a few."

"Great, dear. See you there. If you arrive before me, Duncan's there, so just knock." And with a click, she hung up the call.

Any happiness I felt left me in an instant. I grumbled as I put away my phone. "Duncan's there? Just knock?" I spat out the words. "I've never knocked on that door in twenty-three years. And does she think I've forgotten where she hides the spare key?" I looked at Alex who was pressing his lips together while he listened to me rant. "It's under the stone shaped like a heart next to the maple tree we planted for Grandpa when he passed, by the way," I finished, yelling a little more than I meant to. Hammy sat up and barked, joining in on the game.

"Well, now we're not the only ones who know how to get into your mother's house." Alex glanced over his shoulder. "I'd say pretty much all of campus heard that."

Playfully shoving him, I said, "Good thing it's almost empty right now." Leaning back into him. "I'm sorry, I'm not really handling this all that well."

Alex wrapped his arm around me again, pulling me close. "I can't even imagine my dad meeting someone else, so absolutely no judgments here. I think you're handling it pretty well, to be honest."

There was a short moment where I wished Mom would be more like Alex's dad. But then I remembered *I* wasn't living with her like Alex lived with Detective Valdez, and hadn't since I started college five years ago. I suppose she was bound to get lonely, to want company.

A quote from *Walden* floated on the wind, winding around the tendrils of hair spilling across Alex's shoulder and tickling my cheek. "If we will be quiet and ready enough, we shall find compensation in every disappointment," Thoreau had written.

I thought I would never smile again when I first heard about my dad's heart attack, thought my life would never be as good. But it turned out losing him had given me the push I'd needed to follow in his footsteps and someday become an English professor. It had also put me on the path which led to me getting the bookstore.

And while those things would never be true compensations for what I'd lost—I'd give them all up to have my father back even for a day—I had to admit, things had a way of working themselves out if you let them. Plus, it was nice to see my mom happy again, to catch her eyes light up when she looked at Duncan like they used to when she saw Dad.

I allowed myself to snuggle in close to Alex for a moment before sighing and standing up. "Okay, into the lion's den."

Hammy woke and jumped off the bench, ready at my heels to go wherever our adventures led next. Alex stood and wrapped an arm around my shoulder as we started toward my mother's house… where I would knock, because Duncan was there.

The walk through campus and down Madrona Drive was peaceful, if not a little toasty. Early September in Washington was generally warmer than all of us Pacific Northwesterners were comfortable with, but the knowledge that the rain and snow weren't far away made us feel obligated to enjoy the sunshine while it lasted, no matter how sweaty we got. Alex, however, seemed cool as a cucumber. California summers must've gotten much hotter than this, I supposed.

Finally, we reached my mother's house, my childhood home. The roses Dad had planted along the front of the house were in full bloom still, offsetting the blue of the house with bright yellows and reds, even a few purples. My mother's car wasn't in the driveway, but Duncan's blue BMW was. I repeated Thoreau's words in my head. Despite my outburst, I lifted my hand, made a fist, and knocked on the door. Next to me, Alex cleared his throat and simply put a hand on my lower back in support.

I could hear footsteps thumping on the old wood floors. The sound grew closer and then the door swung open, revealing Duncan. The man looked like a middle-aged movie star, ala George Clooney. He was not very tall, but his full head of salt-and-pepper hair, rugged jawline, and devil-may-care attitude made him look like he was constantly posing for yet another red carpet event or umpteenth gala.

Contrary to his looks, he wasn't a movie star, but had been the manager to a handful of them in Hollywood up until last year when the stress became too much and he decided to move up here. He and my mother hitting it off so well definitely seemed to factor into his decision, but I couldn't blame him for that at all—my mom was beautiful, smart, and powerful in a way which made the people around her feel empowered, too.

"Pepper! Alex! Welcome!" He stepped aside and held a hand out, sweeping it in front of him in a hospitable, be-my-guest kinda way. "Oh, and I can't believe I forgot Hamburger. Hello!" He addressed Hammy as she scrambled in first, her feet slipping on the hardwood.

Gently urging me forward with the hand resting on my back, Alex stepped forward. I let my reservations out in a big sigh and then stepped inside so Duncan could close the door behind us.

I knelt to unclip Ham from her leash. After giving me a thankful snort, she hightailed it over to the large area rug in the living room where her paws had a little more traction.

"Hey, Duncan." I smiled, hoping my expression didn't look as forced as it felt.

I really *had* been getting along with him better lately. After he'd sold his place in California and moved up here for good about six months ago, we'd spent some fun evenings together with my mom, Maggie, Josh, and the kids, as a family. But that was just dinner or a movie or a few rounds of cards. Full-on moving in? This was major stuff.

"Your mom should be here in a few minutes." Duncan checked his watch, his jaw clenching slightly in what I could only assume to be discomfort. "Do you want something to drink while you wait?"

Whenever my mother said she was "just leaving work" it meant she was usually another hour or more out. Call me crazy, but sitting here with a nervous Duncan and an unsure-how-to-handle-it-all Alex for any length of time didn't make the top of my list of things I wanted to do.

"Uh, I can check those boxes now," I said, pointing in the direction of Dad's old study. "If you don't mind me just heading back there," I added, remembering I was supposed to be respecting that this was going to be his house now, too, and that I hadn't lived here for years.

The hard creases in Duncan's camera-ready face softened. "Oh, that's absolutely fine with me." He turned to Alex. "You want anything while the two of us wait?"

Alex's mouth dropped open, but before he could bumble out a response, I grabbed his hand and said, "Oh, I need Alex to help me." I dragged him with me, down the hall before Duncan could argue. Even Hammy abandoned him, noticing we were leaving and following me down the hall in a cacophony of slipping paws and scratching nails.

Ducking into the office which used to house my dad's study behind Hammy and Alex, I closed the door and breathed out a sigh of relief.

"Thank you," Alex whispered, flopping down into the leather armchair in the corner. Ham jumped up and plopped down in his lap.

Winking at him, I plunked down on the floor in front of the first box. Small talk was not one of Alex Valdez's strengths in the best of times, and getting stuck chatting with his girlfriend's mom's boyfriend seemed like a Pit and the Pendulum-level punishment. Undoing the flaps on the box, I peeked in, moving the items on top aside so I could get a good look at the contents.

"So what is all of this?" Alex asked, surveying the half-dozen boxes sitting in various stages of fullness around the room.

"Books mostly," I said, glancing inside the others I could see from where I was sitting.

"And your mom doesn't want them?"

"The only books Mom cares about have titles including the words torts and trials. Plus, she knows I'd probably want most of them, anyway. This is mostly a formality."

"You think you'll sell some of these at the store?" Alex asked.

I hadn't been quite sure of my answer until I felt my nose wrinkle up and my head begin to shake. "I'll keep them in my office in the bookstore for now, since I don't think I can fit anymore in the apartment, but I don't know if I'll be able to let any of them go for a good while."

As I spoke, I lifted a weathered copy of *Walden* out of the mix, resisting the urge to hug it to my chest. Despite the sadness that sat heavy on my chest, making it hard to breathe, a smile tugged at the edges of my mouth.

"There was this one summer when I was…" I paused for a moment, squinting one eye. "Thirteen, I think, and Dad took us all camping." I could almost hear that Tom Petty album start up in my mind like a soundtrack to my memory. "Maggie and Mom wanted to go play at the lake, so Dad and I took a leisurely hike, just the two of us. He brought this and a copy of Thoreau's diary along and read me passages while we walked."

Glancing up, I saw a reminiscent smile grabbing the corners of Alex's lips as well.

"Sounds special. I can see why the book means so much to you, then."

"He *loved* Thoreau." I set the book back down in the box and picked out a thinner volume, *Civil Disobedience*. It was worn, but still maintained, like a chef's favorite knives might be. I thought of Dad's soft voice and wild, unkempt auburn hair. "He used to have this saying when people would tell him he was too quiet to be a redhead. He would say, 'I love being quiet, because it means the majority of people underestimate me and therefore will be wowed when I show them the fire I hold inside.'"

Alex grinned. "Sounds like a quote from Thoreau, honestly." After a moment, he put up his hands and said, "One of the good ones, of course. I don't think everything the guy wrote was awful." He bit at his lip, worry showing in the furrow of his brow.

Laughing, I waved the copy of *Civil Disobedience* at him. "I knew what you meant. Don't worry about it." I flipped open to the title page of the small book. Folding the page back, my eyes caught along the sharp edges of my father's name, marking this as his just like all of the others. But what sat below his name made my heart stop and the breath catch in my throat.

A drawing in the same pen of three As in rotational symmetry, like the top portion of a star.

It felt as if all of the heat was instantly sucked out of my body only to pool in my face, rising up my neck in uncomfortable waves. My rational brain felt like it tumbled into a heap of emotion and confusion.

Had my dad been a TriAlpha?

"Something wrong?" Alex asked.

When I glanced up, he was staring at me, worry evident in his narrowed expression.

"Uh…" I gulped, heart pounding. The book began to slip from my fingers, so I hastily grabbed at it, fumbling as I closed it. "No." Once the lie left my lips, I pressed them together, wishing I could take it back.

But this couldn't be real. My quiet, kind, lovable father couldn't have been involved in this corrupt, haze-happy fraternity.

Alex's eyes searched mine, needing more.

"I—uh—just forgot how intense this one is," I said, willing the heat to leave my cheeks.

He blinked, holding me a few moments more with his gaze, before looking away.

I hastily shoved the book back into the box, folding the flaps back in the crossed pattern so they'd stay closed. Hammy jumped off Alex's lap and began rooting around in the corners of the study, so he moved to sit on the floor next to me. In an effort to take my mind off the symbol, I dug into the next box, smiling over at Alex.

It took us a while to get through the rest, especially since I pulled each book out warily, afraid it might also hold the symbol and I would be forced to acknowledge it was true. Then Alex would know, too. But luckily, the one drawn in Dad's copy of *Civil Disobedience* was the only one of its kind.

My phone buzzed in my pocket, alerting me to an email as I was looking through the penultimate box. Sitting back, I decided to take a break and check the email. I had just found my father's copy of *A Tale of Two Cities* inside and had needed to take a quick cry break anyway. I would've had a hard time seeing one of my favorite books anyway, but with all of the doubts and worries swelling in my heart, it was all that much harder.

Alex took my bout of tears as proof this box was going to come with me and went to add it to the pile while I took my phone out of my pocket. As I turned on the screen and opened my email, my emotions swung from sad to surprise.

"Chloe responded," I said, voice choking around my recent reaction.

Alex turned, eyebrows raised in question. "And?"

I pressed my lips together for a quick second before answering, knowing he wasn't going to like the answer. "She wants to meet at the bookstore, tonight… alone."

11

I knew there was absolutely no way Alex was going to agree to Chloe's stipulation about meeting alone, so when he shook his head and said, "Well that's not happening," I was ready with a plan.

"What if I show up alone…" I started, holding up my finger to stop him when he opened his mouth, an angry scowl darkening his face. "But my super helpful boyfriend chooses that time to drop off these boxes of books." I motioned to the boxes littering my dad's old study, of which I'd decided to take every one.

Alex's eyebrows arched up, showing me he was considering it.

"That way I don't scare her away, but you can still pop in at any moment if you see a need."

He pulled in a deep breath. "Or you could email her back and tell her it was your super helpful boyfriend who found her blog in the first place and really *he* should be the one meeting with her or at least should've been included in the email you sent."

I chuckled, looking at Hammy who'd plopped down

next to me. "Gosh, Ham. With that attitude, no wonder she wanted to meet with me instead." The dog cocked her head to one side and then glanced over at Alex.

He put his hands up. "She didn't—you didn't even let me—" He shook his head. "Fine. We'll do it your way. But I'm coming in with those books the moment I'm uncomfortable with you being alone with her."

Closing the space between us, I stuck out my hand. "Deal."

Alex shook it, rolling his eyes in the process, but I noticed his lips tug into a reluctant smirk. I promptly emailed Chloe back and told her I would meet her at Brooks' Books tonight at five thirty.

Just as I hit send, the sound of the front door opening and closing reverberated through the study. Hammy's ears perked up as my mother's heels clacked against the entryway floors. Glancing down at my watch, I noticed it was nearing two o'clock, which meant she was an hour later than even I had predicted she would be. Alex and I looked at each other. I took one last glance back at the box which held *Civil Disobedience*. I was tempted to take the copy with me so I could investigate its pages further, but I knew after my freak out earlier, Alex would know something was up, so I left it safely tucked away.

Cracking open the door, I let Hammy go first. She was waiting, nose to the opening, butt wagging already, so it was only fair. The knowledge that Ham's adorable antics would temper any mood my mother might be in—depending on what she'd been dealing with at work, the first few minutes after she walked through the front door could vary in intensity—may have factored in my decision, slightly.

Alex and I headed for the living room, but stopped short as we passed by the kitchen, seeing Mom and Duncan in there instead. Mom was leaning down to greet Hammy as Duncan poured her a glass of sparkling water, probably knowing she hadn't hydrated enough while at the office. He timed it perfectly and was proffering it toward her just as she stood up straight, popping the button on her gray suit jacket in a way which was second nature.

Mom took a second to send Duncan an appreciative smile, then she looked to us. "Sorry I'm a little late. I got—"

"Caught up with a case," I said, finishing for her as I walked forward and wrapped her into a hug.

She let out a light laugh, pulling back and touching my cheek with the hand that wasn't gripping her glass as if it were some kind of liquid lifeline. Taking a sip, she raised her eyebrows. "Can you two stay for a late lunch?"

Alex shook his head at the same time I said, "I think we'll pass today. We've got some work to do."

Mom blinked. "Oh? I thought you were on vacation."

"Uh, right. We are, we're just…" I picked at one of my cuticles as I thought of how to describe what we were doing tonight without freaking out my mother.

"Caught up in a case of our own," Alex finished for me, flashing her an "I've got this" grin so Mom wouldn't worry too much about me getting involved in an investigation.

"Alright…" Mom eyed us both cautiously, then glanced down at Hammy as if the dog were involved, too. After a moment, her attention snapped back up to me. "Did you get a chance to check those boxes?"

I nodded, trying my best to hide the way my jaw clenched tight at her apparent eagerness to get rid of all traces of Dad from the house. "Yeah, I'll take anything you don't want," I said, knowing my tone implied the "because I care about him and don't want to get rid of his memory" ending to the sentence without me actually having to say it.

Mom had either missed my snotty tone or she hadn't really been listening to my answer in the first place, because she said, "Good, good. He would've wanted the books to go to you." Her lip quirked up into a small smile. At the same time, her eyes wandered off, far off, past the walls of the kitchen. "It feels like it was yesterday and so long ago all at the same time," she whispered.

My mouth opened slightly and my indignant attitude leaked out of me in a long exhale as I noticed the pain so evident on my mom's face.

Duncan stepped forward, placing a gentle hand on Mom's shoulder, but looking up at me. "A good collection of books your dad had there," he said in a completely obvious "let's change the subject" way.

His words felt like a cold stab in the gut as I thought about the symbol. "You went through them?" I asked, hating the venom so obvious in my tone. Had he seen it? My eyes narrowed at my mother. Did she know?

"Oh—I—not really." He stumbled over his words. "Just glanced at them as I was helping your mother pack up."

Mom sent me a pursed lipped, "Cut it out, Pepper" look.

Before I could say anything else I would regret, I said, "Okay, we've got to get going." I clipped Hammy's leash on to her and grabbed Alex's hand, dragging both of them out of there.

———

STEPPING into my bookstore a few hours later felt like falling into bed at the end of a long, arduous day. The rich smell of paper—new and old—and bindings both cracked and pristine—enveloped me like the best kind of blanket. Once the bell above the door stilled, the place was quiet in that warm, peaceful way. I realized I didn't have to go to a pond to experience a sweet, simple escape like Thoreau. I had it, here.

"Hello! Welcome!" Jess, my only employee said as she poked her head out from behind one of the shelves. "Oh! Pepper, it's you." Her smile widened and she stepped forward, tucking our shop duster into her back pocket. "What happened to camping?"

"Uh… long story," I said, rubbing the back of my neck. "The short of it is there was a murder in the campground and we came home."

Jess's eyes went wide. "Whoa. Intense."

"Right?"

She walked over to the register. "You can still take the time off if you want. I'm fine here. We've been pretty busy, but nothing I can't handle, if you want to recoup."

Jess was about ten years older than me and very much into "self care." Actually, this job was a form of that for her. Her kids were all in school full time now, so she'd decided she wanted to get out of the house.

"Have I told you lately that you're the best?" I smiled at her.

"Almost constantly." She beamed back.

"Well, you are."

It had taken me close to six months to find an employee I trusted enough to leave the shop in their hands, but after going through a few duds, I'd found Jess. She wasn't only efficient and great with customers, but the woman was as committed to hard work as she was to reading at least two books a week.

"And I won't infringe on the full week of work I

promised you," I added. "We wouldn't want you to miss out on those shoes, after all."

Jess had been eyeing these cute flats for weeks. She was hoping to buy with the money she was going to make from the extra hours she would pick up while I was gone camping.

"Shoes *are* very important." She giggled.

"I just have a few things to do here tonight. I'll still pay you for your last hour if you want to go home a little early." I checked my watch, seeing we were about a half hour from closing.

Jess squeezed her shoulders up excitedly. "Well, I won't say no to that." She said hello to Hammy and then grabbed her bag, waving as she left.

Hamburger and I puttered around, reacquainting ourselves with the shop after having been gone for a few days. No other customers came in between the time I took over and when I flipped the sign to "Closed" on the front door.

About five minutes to my meeting time with Chloe, I sequestered Hamburger into my office. I didn't know anything about Chloe besides what she'd written on her blog, and I didn't want Hammy to be involved if this lady was dangerous. As I closed the door, she curled up in her bed and sighed, unhappy about being separated from me, but comfortable and surrounded by chew toys.

I headed back up front to unpack a box of new orders. A few minutes later, I heard knuckles rap on the glass front door. Jumping up, I jogged over to unlock it, letting in a woman about my age. Her straight brown hair flicked around as she glanced to her right and left before coming inside the shop. I eyed Alex's truck parked a few spots down the street. Alex wasn't inside, but sat across the street on a bus bench so he had a better view of me without being too obvious. Closing the door behind Chloe, I turned around. Wild blue eyes met mine.

"Hi there, I'm Pepper. You must be Chloe." I held out my hand, keeping my face soft like my tone, hoping to calm her down.

It didn't seem to work. She gripped my hand with hers for a hot second—and by that, I mean she let go almost immediately and her hand was super sweaty—then paced around my table of new releases near the entrance.

"This is stupid. I shouldn't be doing this." She placed the back of her hand on her forehead. "I just got so excited to hear someone finally believed me, I…" She looked me up and down. "Though, you don't look like you're part of a fraternity."

"Thanks… I think. Do you want to sit down?" I asked, pointing over to the couch and chairs situated around a coffee table toward the back of the shop.

It was a space I'd envisioned small book groups meeting to discuss their favorite fiction, or maybe even a local writers group sharing notes over chapters. I hadn't thought I'd be meeting with a blogger about a secret fraternity in an attempt to find out more about a potential killer. Life was weird.

Chloe sat, but in a way which seemed like she might bolt at any moment, an observation she demonstrated to be valid a few seconds later when there was a knocking on the front door. Chloe shot out of her seat and her eyes darted to me in worry.

"Sorry, it's just my boyfriend dropping off some books. I didn't think he would be here so soon." I tried to keep my teeth from clenching on those last two words as I widened my eyes at Alex through the window. I thought he would let us at least sit for a few minutes before barging in, but I suppose that was the deal I had made.

I walked over to the front door. Throwing the lock, I let Alex in. He had a box of books in his arms and the others were stacked behind him on the sidewalk. At the sight of the boxes, my gut clenched tight all over again, reminded of Dad's book and the symbol he'd sketched inside it. I was also reminded I still hadn't told Alex about what I'd found.

"I—I told you I wanted to meet alone," Chloe said, pulling my attention back.

"Oh, I'm sorry." Alex set down the box then walked over to where Chloe was standing. He held out his hand. "Hey, I'm Alex." From the smooth quality of his voice, I could tell he was putting on the charm, probably even flashing her that dashing Darcy-esque smile of his to put her at ease.

I was about to scoff at his tactics—little did he know I'd already tried all of the smiling niceties—when I heard a giggle flutter out from her. A moment later, she was shaking his hand, holding onto it a lot longer than she had mine. My gaze narrowed. I wanted her to relax, not to develop a crush on my boyfriend.

"Okay, okay." I walked over, grabbing Alex's arm and pulling him away. "I think you have some more boxes to bring in, buddy."

He cocked an eyebrow at me at my use of "buddy," but went back outside to grab the others.

"Sorry." I jabbed a thumb back at him. "He won't bother us anymore." Plopping back onto the couch, I motioned for Chloe to sit again. "Where were we?"

Chloe's eyes widened even more. She sat, but stuttered out, "I—we—should we wait?" Her gaze crept over to where Alex was stacking boxes by the door.

Wrinkling my nose, I waved a hand at her. "Oh, Alex?

Don't worry about him. There's *no* way he's involved in any of this. He's, like, the least likely person to be in a fraternity, ever."

"You trust him?" She leaned in close, whispering.

"Implicitly," I answered without a beat. "He's the one who actually told me about your blog. He believes you, too."

Her shoulders relaxed a few millimeters.

"So tell me how you stumbled onto all of this again," I said, knowing the information would be mostly repeated from her blog. I wanted to see if any part of her story changed.

As Chloe began talking, I noticed Alex nod in approval as he left to grab the last box from the street. *Look at me, using police tactics.* I resisted smiling as I listened. Done with the boxes, Alex relocked the door and came over, standing nearby as Chloe recounted what she'd written in her blog, the only difference being the intense detail in which she went into now we were in person.

Either the girl had memorized the story or it was real, no horse, hound, or turtledove about it.

"You said this Dylan guy told you all about the frat," I said once she'd finished. "Can you share any of that?"

Glancing over at Alex momentarily, Chloe said, "They're called the TriAlphas, Alpha Alpha Alpha. They weren't one of the huge fraternities during the Greek system days here, but they seem to be the only ones who didn't go away when they were outlawed." She swallowed. "I don't know everyone who's in it. He only told me about the main guys."

"The main guys?" Alex asked.

"Dylan said there were a few who seemed to be calling the shots."

"No names?" Alex asked, seeming just as disappointed

as I felt. If Chloe didn't even know who the guys were, how could she have targeted James for revenge?

"No, you'll have to ask Dylan."

"Do you know where we can find him? How we can get ahold of him?" Alex asked, sitting next to me on the couch.

Chloe took a deep breath before reaching out toward a pen and pad of paper sitting on the coffee table. "Yeah, he's going to be mad about me giving you his number, but maybe you guys can talk some sense into him."

Alex raised his eyebrows in question. "I thought you said his goal was to out the fraternity, that he wanted everyone to know who they were and what they were doing?" Alex asked, quoting what Chloe had just told us.

"The past few weeks, he's been so different, really given up hope. I think it's getting to him especially now that school is starting back up, and he got kicked off the baseball team." She shook her head, then finished jotting down his information. She handed the paper over.

I tucked it into my pocket. "Thank you for this."

"I'm just glad someone else believes us." Her weak smile made my heart hurt, but not enough to forget the last question I had for her. "It's been hard feeling like everyone is out to get us, hence my paranoia." A slight blush colored her cheeks.

"Did you at least get to do something fun for the last weekend before fall quarter starts up?" I asked.

Even though Chloe didn't seem to know the identity of any of the guys, it couldn't hurt to get an alibi from her, truly cross her off our suspect list.

Her smile widened a bit. "Yeah, I went to my grandparents' house in Olympia for the weekend. I invited Dylan, but he already had plans with his roommate. He's been really busy lately. We actually haven't been able to hang out as much as we were." She stood, appearing much less manic than when she arrived.

Olympia was at least three hours from the campground. Well, there was her alibi, and Dylan's too, apparently.

"Oh, wow. Inviting him to your grandparent's. You two are really close then?"

She blushed. "We're dating actually." Her eyes widened, and the slight pink in her cheeks turned red. "But that's not why I wrote the blog. We didn't start dating until weeks after it published. When you're the only two people who know the truth about something, it really brings you together."

Her defensiveness about the subject piqued my interest. That definitely seemed like a sore subject, but by the way she was standing and inching closer to the door, it appeared she was done talking.

"Thank you for talking to me." I stood as well. "Us," I added, as Alex followed.

"You guys be careful," Chloe said, her blue eyes darkening for a moment. "These guys are no joke and their influence seems to know no limits. I swear they got to campus security when I went to talk to them, not to mention getting Dylan kicked off the team."

"We will be," Alex said.

We walked her to the door, waving goodbye.

Once she was out of sight, I pulled out my phone. "So call Dylan?"

Alex snatched it from my hand. "Yes, but this time, I get to be the one to set up the meeting." He grinned as I handed over the paper with Dylan's number and went to let Hammy out of the office.

12

I sipped at my mocha truffle frap as I stared at the front door of Bittersweet the next day. Alex sat next to me, sipping on his own drink—just a black coffee, though, not fun at all. Only five minutes until nine in the morning, Dylan was set to come through those doors at any moment.

Admittedly, I was slightly disappointed with him being okay with meeting in a crowded, public place—I'd been looking forward to finding a way to come "rescue" Alex like he had for me with Chloe. But any disappointment melted away when I realized meeting at Bittersweet meant I would get to have one of Nate's awesome experimental fraps while I waited. The truffle frap I was blissfully consuming had homemade chocolate syrup as well as caramel and chocolate drizzle. It was heaven on crushed ice.

"Is the taste satisfactory?" Nate asked, slinking up behind me, seemingly out of nowhere.

Eyes wide, I pointed to the long drag I was taking on the straw. Once I swallowed, I said, "Omigosh, I don't ever want to stop drinking; it's so good."

A smile curled onto Nate's face. He'd been known as the

town career-nomad up until a couple of years ago when he bought Bittersweet, selling vacuums one week and then sketchy insurance the next. We all thought the café was going to be just another one of his ill-fated, money-making schemes and would fizzle out in a month or two. But the man actually had a talent for slinging espresso shots and for coming up with delicious latte concoctions.

"Seriously, Nate," I continued. "This is so good, I kinda want to marry it."

Alex cleared his throat, next to me, arching one eyebrow.

"Uh, if I weren't already in a committed relationship, that is."

"With a human," Alex added.

"Sure, sure. The human part." I waved a hand at him and stuck the straw back in my mouth.

"Oh, good news," Nate said. Before I had a chance to look up at him, a large blade snicked open inches away from my face.

I sucked in a surprised gulp of air and frap, coughing as the icy drink invaded my trachea. Putting up my free hand as a lame defense, I scooted my chair back a few inches.

"The sheriff called yesterday and said my knife was cleared. Drove out last night to get it back," Nate finished, none-the-wiser that he'd just about scared all of the caffeine out of my body.

Alex cleared his throat, but it seemed more to get Nate's attention than out of sympathy for me. He gave his head a quick shake and narrowed his eyes at Nate, who seemed to get the hint because he folded the blade down and tucked the knife back into his pocket.

I continued to cough the last bits of offensive material

from my windpipe as Nate wandered back toward the register to join Victoria. She gave me a sheepish wave as a few new customers had walked in. I returned her wave, then directed it at the locals who'd just walked in. Following closely behind them were two college-aged guys, one with sandy-blond hair and another with dark brown. They were both on the shorter side, just a few inches taller than me. The blond man locked eyes on Alex right away. Dylan Oakes. He strode over to our table and pulled up a chair. His friend broke off from him, heading straight for the counter to order.

Armed with the knowledge we were meeting in public, I already expected Dylan's paranoia level to be much lower than Chloe's. But I hadn't expected the impassive guy who dropped into the chair across from us. He didn't even glance around the coffee shop to make sure none of the frat members were present—none were, by the way, of the ones I could identify… I'd checked.

"Thanks for meeting with us," Alex said.

Dylan shrugged. "Not sure what good it'll do."

"We'd like to ask you a few questions about TriAlphas, if you don't mind." Alex leaned forward, setting his coffee on the table.

Dylan narrowed his eyes. "I think I deserve to ask a few questions, first."

I could feel Alex adjust his position in his seat next to me. Chloe had warned us Dylan would be different, but I guess neither of us had expected the cagey attitude we were getting at the moment. From the way he pulled in a long breath, I could tell Alex was about to say something intense and cop-level authoritative.

Placing a hand on my boyfriend's arm, I smiled at Dylan. "You sure you don't want to get something to drink first?" I asked, holding mine up as a display. "Nate makes a mean frap."

Dylan scanned the menu hanging above the counter. "Uh, yeah. I'll grab something, sure."

As soon as he was gone, I leaned over and whispered, "How much can we tell him? Legally?"

Alex pressed his lips together, tight. "We shouldn't say anything about the way James died or the journal he left behind, but other than that, everyone will know soon enough James has been killed."

I nodded, hoping sharing that fact might help us answer his questions, the first of which I anticipated would be, "Why do you suddenly care about this?"

"I'd like to share as little as we can, though," Alex said.

"Of course." I dipped my chin seriously as if it weren't my usual modus operandi to blurt out information about cases and sometimes even accusations.

A few moments later, Dylan settled back into his chair with his own frap in hand. His friend had settled at a small two-top next to us, and he pulled out a paperback, opening it to a page in the center. Focusing back on Dylan, I beamed at the fact he'd taken my suggestion. *Okay*, I thought. *This guy may be a bit salty, but I can get through to him.*

"Which one did you get?" I asked, holding my own frap to my lips and taking a satisfying sip.

Dylan squinted one eye. "Uh, something with peppermint, I think."

"The Thin Mint?" I let out a little gasp. Nate's Girl-Scout-cookie-inspired frap had a homemade peppermint simple syrup as well as real pieces of the cookies inside. I leaned forward as he took his first sip. Then his eyes lit up, lips pulling into the first smile I'd seen him make.

"If we're done discussing drinks…" Alex said, looking from Dylan to me.

"Right, your questions." I pushed my shoulders back, ready.

Dylan licked his lips. "Why now? If you believe Chloe and me, why did it take you so long to contact us?"

Glancing at Alex, I tipped my head in his direction, letting him take the lead on this.

"We only realized the frat was around this weekend, through… other means. Chloe's blog confirmed our suspicions."

I bit my lip, impressed with Alex's ability to say something without really saying anything.

"You working with them?" Dylan fired his second question at us right away.

His question reminded me about my father, about how it was possible he had been one of them, working with them. A terrible, tightness crept up my throat. I noticed that his friend glanced up from his book for a brief second, telling me he was definitely listening in.

Deciding to take the lead on this one, I shook my head fervently. "Absolutely not," I croaked around the unanswered questions closing around my throat. "We want them to answer for the people they've hurt."

Ironically—despite his frosty beverage—Dylan seemed to thaw a little at my statement. He took another sip of his frap.

"Any more questions?" Alex asked.

Dylan shrugged. "Maybe. I'll let you know. For now, you can ask a few."

"How well did you get to know them?" Alex asked, not wasting a moment.

"Pretty well. Rush week was almost over when I had the accident, so I'd spent a lot of time with them by the end."

Scrunching one eye, I was about to argue that taking a dozen shots—or however many the guy had to have consumed in order to give himself alcohol poisoning—was rarely an accident, but I kept my mouth shut. We needed Dylan's information if we had any hope of narrowing down our list of secret-frat suspects.

"Did you notice any problems between group members?" Alex asked. "Any fighting?"

Pulling in a deep breath, Dylan tipped his head to the left as he looked up at the ceiling. "Uh, yeah. A heck of a lot of it, actually."

I scooted closer, sipping on my frap with a renewed gusto.

"The president, James, pretty much pissed people off like it was his job."

"The other guys didn't like him?" Alex took my cue and leaned forward, too, lowering his voice.

"I wouldn't say that. It was more like the guy was Caesar or something. They spent half their time worshiping him and the other half all mad about how bossy he was being. I could totally see them stabbing him in the back if they got the chance, but then they would hold a funeral for the guy right after they killed him talking about what a great man he was. You know."

My shoulders scrunched up in excitement and I glanced at Alex.

"Uh oh," he said. "You did it now. Mentioning Shake-speare around this one usually earns you a lengthy literary discussion, complete with quotes."

Placing a hand over my chest, I feigned a pained look of surprise. "Et tu, Alex?"

He laughed and said, "See?"

Dylan, whom I was quickly warming to, laughed as well. If he only knew how right he was about James's tragic end.

"Anyone stand out as a Brutus?" I asked.

"Of course. In the same position, too." Dylan took another drink of his frap. "Matt, his right hand man or vice president seemed to get in a fight with James every time we all got together. And when he wasn't fighting with the guy, he was talking about him behind his back, telling the other guys he would make a much better president."

Alex's forehead wrinkled as he thought. "Did anyone talk about James wanting to move the frat to Southern Washington University?"

"Yep. James was trying to convince everyone it was a good idea. They've got a Greek system down there, so he thought it would be better for the TriAlphas than trying to remain underground. He was sick of hiding, wanted to be a part of something he could brag about, I think."

I sighed, knowing that sentiment could very well be why he was now dead. "Fools stand on their island of opportunities and look toward another land. There is no other land; there is no other life but this," I said, quoting Thoreau.

Dylan's friend shifted in his seat.

Alex shook his head. "Can't we be done with Thoreau?"

"Oh god, yeah," Dylan said. "Thoreau was all those guys talked about. Except James. He didn't seem as mad about the guy or his book as the rest of them. Told me he thought the guy was a quack."

"Odd that the leader of the organization would be openly critical of the person they mirrored most of their beliefs around," I said, feeling confusion catch in the creases between my eyebrows. It didn't sound like the James I knew from the pages of his journal.

"Yeah. Well, I don't think moving the frat was the only change James wanted to make." Dylan lifted one shoulder then let it drop.

"What do you mean?" I asked.

"Got the impression James wanted a more quintessential fraternity experience, is all. He's the first one to involve hazing in the rushing process."

"So Matt seemed particularly violent toward James," Alex mused. "Anyone else?"

"I heard some stuff about a few alumnus being pretty vocal against the move." Dylan stopped, narrowing his eyes as he thought. "They almost seemed to care more than current members."

"Loyalty is a pretty good motive," I mumbled, thinking of my father. If he really was a member, he hid it well. And if all of them were that good at concealing their involvement, there could be any number of past members out there.

Dylan narrowed his eyes. "Motive for what?" He sat up. "What's this all about anyway?"

I could see the muscles in Alex's jaw clench tight. Crap. I wasn't supposed to say anything if we could avoid it. I must've gotten caught up in thoughts about Dad and hadn't realized what I was saying.

"There's been a death in the group," Alex said reluctantly.

At this, Dylan's friend closed his book and turned toward us.

Blinking, Dylan let out a whoosh of breath. He met his friend's surprised gaze, then looked back at us. "They had another rush this soon? During the summer?" He sighed. "I guess my group was too much of a disappointment."

Wrinkling my nose, I looked away, not wanting to give anything else away.

But I needn't have worried, because Alex said, "Not another rush. One of the standing members was murdered."

Eyes wide, Dylan sat forward. "No way. They offed one of their own?"

The fact that he'd jumped to the conclusion that one of the frat members had to be to blame if another one had died didn't escape me, but I decided to tuck it away for now.

"Literally," I said. When Dylan glanced at me in question, I added, "They were off in the woods when said offing happened." I turned my attention to Dylan's friend. "You can join us, you know."

The guy was leaning so much that I was afraid his chair was going to topple right over.

His cheeks reddened and he smiled nervously. "Sorry." He stood, moving his stuff to our table. "I'm Liam, Dylan's roommate. I didn't mean to eavesdrop, I've just heard all about these guys…"

Dylan nodded. "Now your questions make a lot more sense. You're trying to figure out who did it." After a second, the understanding left his face, replaced with scrunched confusion. "Wait, why are *you guys* involved?"

"We were camping next to them when it happened," Alex said. "And this one has a bit of a Nancy Drew complex." He jabbed a thumb in my direction, chuckling to show he was teasing.

"Plus," I said, shooting Alex a fake scowl, "there's a completely incompetent sheriff dealing with the case, and we don't trust him to investigate."

Dylan exhaled. "Got it. Well, be careful." His gaze landed on me for a moment. "Especially you." When I twisted my mouth into a confused frown, he elaborated. "James has a thing for redheads. He'll definitely notice you if you're snooping around."

I remembered back to our first day at the campsite, when James had winked at me. My stomach churned and I realized all too late that I'd given something away.

Dylan blinked. "No way. So they really did stab Caesar?" He exhaled a quick, humorless laugh. "Man, I guess it's not really a surprise, but… wow."

His redhead comment made me think about the journal note about Kevin and James fighting over the same girl. "What about Kevin? You think he could've done it?" I asked Dylan. I knew Kevin was definitely taller than James, so it was very unlikely that he was the killer, but it didn't hurt to ask.

"No." He cut the air with one hand. "He was totally a Mark Antony. They got in fights now and then, but he would never have done anything to hurt James. At least from what I could see." He shifted his feet on the tiled floor of the coffee shop. "No, if James is dead, your man is undoubtedly Matt. He's your Brutus, for sure."

Going over Chloe's article in my head, I thought of one more thing I wanted to ask Dylan about. "When you were hanging out with them, did any of them talk about Ethan Emsworth? I know Chloe had stipulated that Ethan may have been involved with the fraternity when he passed aw—"

Interrupting me, Dylan shook his head and said, "Look, as interested as I am in seeing these guys suffer, I told myself I wouldn't let them ruin any more of my days. I think I've had enough." His cagey attitude from earlier returned.

Alex and I glanced at each other as Liam and Dylan moved to leave.

"Just one more thing," Alex said, his words causing Dylan to stop. "Where were you this weekend?"

Dylan cocked an eyebrow at the question for a moment. "You ask Chloe the same question?" he asked.

Alex sat in silence, watching him. When Dylan seemed to understand Alex wasn't going to answer that question, his eyes flashed over to Liam and they shared a quick look I couldn't read. Then, just when I thought he was going to tell Alex to go shove it, he cleared his throat and answered, "Liam and I were at our apartment the whole weekend, playing video games."

Alex looked to Liam, who dipped his chin in confirmation.

"The whole weekend?" Alex asked.

"Uh, yeah. All of it." Liam cleared his throat.

Dylan laughed. "You know how Black Ops can be." The roommates high-fived and it was apparent from the look on my boyfriend's face that no, he didn't.

With a sigh, Alex waved them off. We sat in silence as they left.

Once they were out the door, however, my attention flew to Alex. "Well, that seems to fit with what Chloe told us."

Running his palm over the stubble on his chin, he narrowed his eyes.

"What? You think he's lying?" I asked, feeling like there was definitely something off about his alibi.

"Someone is."

A lex dropped me off at the apartment after our meeting with Dylan with promises to talk with his father about the possibility of Dylan's alibi being… off. He was also going to ask the detective whether or not there was enough evidence to bring in Matt for questioning.

"It's a sensitive matter since this is technically still in Sheriff Langley's hands. Dad will know the questions to ask and how to handle it," Alex assured me when I asked why I couldn't be a part of it. "Plus, he's at the station right now, so we have to wait until he gets home. I was going to fit in a quick run in the meantime, if you want to come with."

My nose wrinkled up instinctually. "A run? Uh… maybe I'll see what Liv is up to." I kissed him and scrambled out of the truck toward the apartment before I was roped into doing any exercise.

Alex laughed and put his hand up in a wave as he pulled away.

I dug out my keys and headed inside. I could do with some girl time, anyway.

The only girl inside was Hamburger—happy to see me

but, admittedly, not the best conversationalist. After kissing, hugging, patting, and playing a bit of tug of war, I pulled out my phone and texted Liv.

Where you at?

She responded right away.

Grammar much, English major?

I scoffed before typing, *Uh… on vacation.*

She sent back a smiley face and then added, *At the campus library.*

Workaholic, I typed back, knowing it had to be why she was there. She worked in the business office on campus, and I knew if she went in on a day off, they would give her a hard time. Before I could respond, telling her I was coming to join her, she sent another message.

Oh. Guess who's back in town? A moment later, a picture came through, obviously sneakily snapped over the top of her book. It was Kevin from the TriAlphas with his arm wrapped around a pretty young woman.

Wow, I think I've really underestimated these frat guys' commitment to the written word. Between their obsession with Thoreau, to Dylan's use of Julius Caesar analogies, and now Kevin hanging out in the library before the quarter even started, I had to admit they were seeming like a downright scholarly bunch.

Uh. Well, they just went back to Small, Dark, and Red, so I'm not sure it's the written word he's after, Liv responded.

Small, Dark, and Red—as I liked to refer to the secluded two-seater in the back corner of the library because of its diminutive lamp with a sexy red shade—was a known make-out spot. In fact, it had been the place Alex and I had first kissed almost two years earlier, when we were still figuring out our feelings toward each other.

I named all of the sitting areas in the library based on

the unique lamp which resided there. In fact, from the picture she sent me, I could tell Liv was sitting in Fringy Pink, a leather chaise-type lounge with a pink, fringe-hemmed lamp standing guard. It was the perfect summer reading spot because it was situated right next to a tall window looking out on a beautiful red-budded rhododendron. The perfect mix of sun and shade.

Make room in Fringy Pink for me. I'm on my way!

Liv responded with a thumbs-up. I took Hammy on a short walk, then grabbed my father's copy of *Walden*—having pulled it from the box yesterday before I'd left the bookshop—and headed to the library.

It was only a five-minute walk from our place, so I arrived before I could work up a sweat in the midmorning sunshine. Before going to Fringy Pink to meet up with Liv, I skirted through the aisles of books and made my way silently back toward Small, Dark, and Red. I slowed my feet as I approached, the sound of sniffling stopping me completely a few feet from the edge of the row so I was just out of their line of sight.

"I can't believe he's gone," a young woman said, her voice wobbly with tears. "We only just started dating."

Dating? Had this girl been James's girlfriend?

"I know. It's surreal. I keep expecting him to show up," Kevin said. There was a shuffling of fabric as if he was moving, probably moving closer given their location. "Don't worry, though. We'll make it through this, together."

Yeah, it sounded like Kevin was putting the moves on her.

"We're having a little get-together tomorrow night at the house. You should come. I'll text you the details. And if we don't answer the front door…" Kevin whispered the rest, so I couldn't hear.

Peeking in between the tops of books and the shelf, I tried to get a look at the couple, but all I could see was long, auburn hair. Dylan's comment about James's interest in redheads this morning jumped into my mind.

"Will Matt be there?" she asked after a few moments and a sniffle.

Kevin scoffed. "Psh. I don't know. The jerk was gone all last night, didn't return any of our calls."

"Kev, that's not good."

I heard the rustle of clothing and then Kevin said, "Don't you worry about him, beautiful. Honestly, we're better off without Matt. I'm still not convinced he isn't the reason James is gone."

She gasped. "That's an awful thing to say!"

"Why? It's the truth. Probably won't answer any of our calls because he skipped out, ran away to Canada or something."

I sucked in a quick breath at Kevin's statement.

"Did you hear something?" he asked and then I heard him stand.

Scuttling away, I headed toward the north end of the library where Liv was reclined in the chaise with her laptop balanced on her knees. When she noticed me, she lifted up her legs to make room. I tucked myself into the vacated spot before she lowered her legs back down, knees bent up like a bridge over me.

"How are Kevin and his lady-friend?" she asked without taking her eyes off the screen.

The girl knew me too well.

"Crying," I said.

Liv looked up from her laptop, interest written on her face as plain as the document open in front of her.

"I think it might be the girl James was seeing, but Kevin sure seems interested."

"Do you think this could've been a case of him offing the competition?"

Sighing, I said, "I don't know. Alex and I met with Dylan this morning and he seemed adamant Kevin was definitely on Team James. Plus, the guy is tall, taller than James was for sure. I don't think he's our guy."

"Yeah, and killing someone over a college crush seems a little intense."

"A little." I nodded.

We sat in silence for a moment or two, and then Liv got sucked back into her work so I pulled out a book and became enveloped by Thoreau's life in the woods.

The clicking of heels across the wood floors of the library pulled my attention up a while later. I could feel Liv shift and look up, too. We glanced from the auburn-haired girl to each other then back to her, walking out of the library. Alone. No Kevin draped over her this time.

One look back at Liv and I could see her expression narrow in the same way mine probably had. Without talking, we got up from our comfy position, quickly gathering our stuff. We shuffled through the aisles of books until we were close to the back corner. Tiptoeing the rest of the way, we crept over to the spot between the books and the shelf where we might be able to see Small, Dark, and Red.

Although I could only catch a glimpse, I was fairly certain it was Kevin. He'd stayed behind. And if Dylan was right, if Kevin really was loyal to James, maybe he could give us some insight into who in the group might be the killer.

Liv and I could either communicate telepathically after living together for this long, or our brains just came up with the same half-baked plans at the same time. She nudged me forward, nodding toward the empty seat across from him. I leaned around the shelf, making sure it really was him before committing.

He sat there, head cradled in his hands, letting it rock back and forth slowly. I cleared my throat. Kevin glanced up, blinking bleary-eyed.

"Hey there…" I stepped forward and felt Liv follow behind. "I don't know if you remember us…"

His face contorted into a scowl. I was about to turn and bolt, to push Liv away whispering, "Abort, abort" when Kevin's face softened, even turned up into a smile.

"Oh yeah. From the campground." He sat all the way up.

"Care if we join you?" I asked, gesturing to the empty chair across from him, not the one he'd pulled up next to him to better cuddle with the redhead.

"Sure." He pointed to the chair next to him and looked at Liv as I plopped myself into the seat farthest away.

Right after my butt hit the cushion, Liv's hip shoved me to the side until I had one cheek on, one off. "Thanks, but we're fine sharing."

I leaned forward. "How are you doing?"

"Not great, to be honest," he said.

"Well, that's completely understandable." Liv widened her eyes. "What happened to your friend was awful. Not to mention one of your friends could possibly be the killer." She kept cool even when Kevin coughed in surprise.

The woman was a genius.

Finally acknowledging his reaction, Liv leaned forward. "I mean, do you think so?"

Kevin licked his lips, then swallowed and sighed. "I guess."

"Who does the sheriff think it could be?" I asked, wondering if Kevin knew any more about the sheriff's suspect list than we did.

"He told us these things take time, they might not even have a list of suspects for a few days. I mean, they questioned all of us, and the rest of the campers, but…" he shrugged. "We haven't heard anything more."

Feigning ignorance, I said, "Didn't he get in a fight with one of the guys in your group the night he was killed?"

"Yeah, Matt." Kevin's posture visibly stiffened. His face darkened just as it had when we'd been sitting around drinking coffee the other morning.

"And do you think Matt is capable of doing… that to someone?" Liv asked, cringing at her inability to describe the murder in any detail.

I held my breath as Kevin paused.

"Psh. Totally. It wouldn't surprise me at all. I'm so sick of the guy, honestly. He's really hot-tempered and is always starting fights with everyone we hang out with, especially James. He and James—well, the fight they got in that night was pretty nasty. I was wasted, but I can't think of anyone else who left the campsite as long as Matt did, either."

That was it, confirmed by one of their own. Matt had motive and opportunity. Now to find out about means.

"The sheriff took the knives we brought for cooking into evidence. Did he take anything from you guys?" I asked, trying to keep my voice calm lest it reveal my interest in this, the last piece I needed.

"Yeah, a few of us had pocket knives. Others had scarier hunting knives, you know, in case we saw any bears."

I was about to mention I didn't think a hunting knife was going to do much to protect you from live bears, especially when you were drunk, but I kept that tidbit to myself. I needed Kevin to feel comfortable enough to keep talking and he was already starting to squirm, glance around, look for a way out.

"Were there any knives missing?" I chewed on my lip as I willed him to hang on for just a few more questions.

At this, Kevin's face tightened. "Matt's. He was showing it off earlier in the day, throwing it into trees and pretending to cut people. When the sheriff came and asked, Matt didn't hand anything in and he gave us all a threatening look like we shouldn't say anything." Kevin scoffed. "Typical Matt. Running around, doing whatever he wants without consequences. When the sheriff left, Matt told us he couldn't find it, but it wasn't a big deal, he would just buy another one. Brushed it off."

"And you didn't think that was important to tell the sheriff?" Liv asked, ineffectively concealing the incredulity in her tone.

Her question did bring to mind many of my own. Namely, what if they didn't say anything because they actually worked together to kill James? What if there wasn't just one killer, but a whole group?

"I told you, Matt's a pretty scary guy. Super intense," Kevin answered, breaking my chain of thought.

"Yeah, and possibly a killer," I said. "You need to say something to the sheriff."

Kevin clenched his jaw.

"Like today," Liv added.

Finally, he dipped his head once. "Okay. I'll call when I get home." He stood, giving us a defeated wave.

Liv and I said goodbye. Once we got up and checked that he was really out of earshot, I grabbed Liv's arms at the same moment she whispered, "Did that just happen?"

"We have to call Alex right now." I let go of Liv and

called him up, tapping my foot while the dial tone buzzed in my already buzzing head.

"Hey, I was just about to—"

"Matt did it," I whispered as forcefully as I could, aware we were still in the library. "Liv and I just ran into Kevin and he told us Matt had a big hunting knife with him at the campground, which he said he lost, but didn't tell the sheriff about." I paused to breathe. "He had motive, means, and opportunity, Alex. It's got to be him."

Alex cleared his throat. "I don't think it is, Pepper."

"Why? How? Everything points straight to—"

"He's in intensive care at the hospital right now. Someone tried to kill him last night."

14

"Wh-what?" I stammered, louder than I should've in the library. The shelves of books swirled around me.

Liv's eyes searched my face, obviously unaware of the bomb Alex had just dropped on me, the wrench he'd thrown into our theory.

"What happened?" I asked again.

"Someone jumped him last night when he was walking back from a bar."

"Do you think it was the same person?"

Liv frowned next to me, slowly figuring out what happened based on my end of the conversation.

"I don't know. They didn't slit his throat, but they did beat him within an inch of his life. I'm sure whomever did it thought he was dead, but the guy's tough. He hung on long enough for morning when someone found him in an alley, barely breathing."

I sucked in a quick breath at the details. "That's awful." I could feel the creases in my forehead deepening as I thought of how angry Kevin seemed with Matt. "You don't think maybe someone was trying to get back at him for killing James, do you?" I asked.

"We can't rule it out, of course. But I think it might also mean this wasn't an inside job."

"Dylan or Chloe." I said, thinking of the weirdness with Dylan's alibi.

"Chloe's out. Dad checked in on her alibi and her grandparents said she was there all weekend."

Which meant Dylan might still be a suspect. I nodded, then remembered Alex couldn't see me through the phone. "Okay, is there anything you want me and Liv to do?"

"Stay safe, get home if you can. I don't know if Kevin is involved in this or not, but if he is, he has good reason to think you two are snooping around now that you two just questioned him."

"Got it." I swallowed, checking over my shoulder, heart-beat quickening. Alex was right. What I thought had been an awesome catch on our part now felt incredibly danger-ous. "We're leaving now."

"I'll call in a little bit, when I know more," Alex said, his tone softening.

"We still on for our Alex and Pepper day tomorrow?" I asked. Seeing as how we'd missed out on most of our camping trip, we'd decided to go for a long hike, just the two of us, to make up for the time lost.

"Absolutely. Wouldn't miss it."

After hanging up, Liv and I hustled ourselves out of the library and I filled her in on what Alex had told me while we made the short trip home—only stopping for a minute at the minimart on the corner to grab a few pints of ice-cream. We stayed inside the rest of the day, trying to beat the heat by stuffing cool, creamy spoonfuls into our mouths and watching some good ol' romantic comedies.

Alex called during our second movie, telling me he'd be there to pick me up at eight in the morning, sharp, which really meant seven-fifty in Alex time.

———

DESPITE FEELING a bit sluggish from the early departure time, and the too-much-ice-cream hangover I was nursing, I was ready by fifteen-minutes-to-eight the next morning.

I was taking Hammy on her morning constitutional when a car honk made me jump nearly out of my skin. Hammy barked, racing around me in circles I think were meant to protect me, but really just served to wrap me up in her leash so I was trapped, easy prey for whatever honking foe I was about to face.

Because, really, what kind of person honked at people this early in the morning? They had to be bad news.

Untangling myself, I glanced up. The honking seemed to have come from a dark SUV with mobster-level tinted windows. Definitely not Alex. I turned to walk away, willing Hammy to pee as I pointed us on a course to our front door. The buzzing sound of an automatic window lowering caught my ear and slowed my steps, but I kept going, sending out a silent plea for the car to just leave.

"Morning, beautiful." A voice called out, stopping me in my tracks.

Alex.

Upon hearing his voice, Hammy began dragging me closer to the SUV. When we were about five feet away, I was able to pick up the little monster. She snorted and paddled

ERYN SCOTT

her legs in the air in an effort to get closer to Alex's hand extending from the passenger window.

"Hey." I giggled as he pet Hamburger. "I was expecting you to come in the truck."

It was then that my brain began to register the fact Alex was in the passenger seat, not the driver's. Blinking, I leaned to the side to get a look past him. His father sat behind the wheel, sunglasses on, smirk evident. He lifted his hand in a wave.

"Oh! Hi, Detective."

"Miss Brooks."

"Sorry, but Dad thought we should go pay the sheriff visit. I know we were supposed to have our day today, but… do you mind putting it on hold until we finish with this case?"

My heart dropped a bit, but instead of letting him cancel on me, a plan came to mind. "Sure." I pointed to Hammy. "I've still gotta get this little lady to pee and then we can hit the road," I said, inviting myself along, even though I knew it wasn't his intention. I wasn't about to be left behind.

Detective Valdez opened his mouth, like he was going to say something, but Alex interrupted him.

"Take your time." He winked at me, then pulled his hand away from Hammy so I could set her down.

Because she's a show off, Ham did her business right away, despite having put me through five minutes of her smelling everything in sight before the Valdez men arrived. Popping back inside, I unclipped her leash and yelled, "See you later," to Liv.

She poked a towel-wrapped head out from her room. "Good luck. Have fun on your Pepper and Alex day. Ham and I will hold down the fort."

I pulled in a long breath through my teeth. "Well, he has to do something with his dad and I sorta just invited myself along, which I don't think the detective is too happy about, so…"

"Yikes. Well, maybe just the good luck part." Liv winked.

"Thanks."

Grabbing my purse and sunglasses, I walked out into the morning sunshine. The passenger door opened and Alex stepped out. He opened the backseat door for me and then moved like he was going to follow me inside.

"Wait, what are you doing?" I asked, stopping mid-scoot.

"I didn't want you to feel like a criminal riding in the backseat, so I thought I would ride back here with you." He blinked.

I officially had the sweetest boyfriend, but there was no way I was going to make the detective drive us around chauffeur-style. I placed a hand on Alex's chest and pushed him back.

"Uh-uh. I'm fine. You ride up there with your dad. I promise I don't feel like a criminal, especially since this car doesn't have one of those cages separating the front and back."

Alex exhaled, but put his hands up and then climbed back into the passenger seat.

"Plus," I said, leaning a forearm on each of the front seats, "this way I can be here in between you two and whisper classic literature quotes in your ears while we drive." I laughed, but immediately regretting suggesting I would whisper anything into my boyfriend's father's ear.

This was going to be a *long* drive.

"Just kidding." I laughed again, too loud this time. "Of

course I wouldn't lean forward like that, because it would mean I wasn't wearing my seatbelt. Which I *always* do, for the record." Catching the detective's eye in the rear view mirror, I gave him a wink and a two fingered salute like some sort of pilot.

Alex glanced back at me, pressing his lips together in a "you feeling okay?" look.

I just shook my head, searching for some duct tape to place over my mouth while I buckled myself in, or maybe there was a blanket I could drape over my head until we got there. An hour each way. I exhaled and sat back.

Detective Valdez looked over at Alex, then back at me to check we were buckled and then he put the SUV into drive, pulling out of my apartment complex parking lot.

"This is a nice car. Super fancy," I said, running my hand along the immaculate cloth backseats. "Is it yours or the department's?"

I realized I'd never actually noticed what kind of car the detective drove. He was one of those odd people who actually parked his car inside his garage, and I wasn't one to snoop around Alex's house—well, not while he was there, at least.

"It's mine as long as I work on the force," the detective answered. "Detectives are usually issued unmarked vehicles, but it still has all of the bells and whistles." As if to prove it, he pushed a few buttons, eliciting a quick burst of sirens and flashing lights.

"Oh!" My eyes widened. "I bet that person just about peed their pants," I said, pointing to the car turning in front of us.

Alex laughed.

My body relaxed back into the seat. Detective Valdez

seemed a little more laid back than he had when I'd first invited myself along. Maybe this trip wouldn't be so bad.

"Alex filled me in on the conversation you two had with Dylan Oakes yesterday, but I'd like to hear what you learned from Kevin Thomas, if you don't mind humoring me."

I didn't and so I told the detective, and Alex who hadn't heard all of the details yet either, about how Kevin had implicated Matt as the murderer, about his missing knife, and about him being the only one who left the site for a long period of time after James went missing.

"But," I said, wrapping up, "none of that really seems important now Matt's been attacked, too."

"It does seem to point at someone outside of the group, since Matt seemed to represent an opposite opinion to all of the issues which caused disagreements between the members and James," the detective said, keeping his eyes on the road.

"Right. Anyone who was mad at James's efforts to move the frat would've had no cause to hurt Matt, since he wanted it to stay," Alex said.

It seemed like our options there were now even more limited.

We sat in frustrated silence for a few miles, but eventually Detective Valdez asked me to explain how fraternities came to be banned at NWU. That ended up taking the majority of the rest of the drive, as it was a long and arduous process, spurred ahead by the tragic deaths of three pledges during a particularly gruesome rush week. While neither Maggie nor I had been born when the whole thing had gone down, Dad had actually been a student there during the ban. That plus my family had always been very involved in the university—Dad going on to be a professor there and my mom an appointee on the board of regents on multiple occasions—so I heard stories about everything university related.

"The most confusing part is that I don't even remember hearing about Alpha Alpha Alpha during any of my parents' stories. They definitely weren't one of the bigger fraternities. If they had been, I'm sure their symbol or their name would've rung some kind of bell."

The SUV continued to climb up the foothill switch-backs, the trees getting thicker as the roads turned from back highways to dirt single-car tracks.

"Thank you for the information, Pepper. It definitely helps give me a bigger picture." Detective Valdez cleared his throat. "Okay. Before we arrive, we need to talk about our plan."

I straightened. This sounded like serious business. I leaned forward.

"I've called Sheriff Langley and told him about Matt Kincaid's condition. He knows that if what happened to Matt and James is linked, this case is not only in his jurisdiction. Unlike me, he's not convinced there is a connection, so I expect quite a bit of pushback from him."

Alex and I nodded.

"Alex, your job will be to get copies of the ranger's registration books from the weekend. I want Friday especially." He glanced over at his son.

"Got it."

"I'll tackle the sheriff and see if I can get him to share any evidence he's collected thus far."

"How do you know he'll be there?" I asked, assuming we were going to the campground and not to the sheriff's office down the valley.

Detective Valdez exhaled. "He's hiding something. If we're snooping around, he'll be there for sure."

I pressed my lips together, wondering if he'd forgotten to give me a job. Who was I kidding? He wouldn't be giving me a job. Of course he wouldn't. I wasn't a part of th—

"And Pepper," he said, interrupting my thoughts.

"Yeah." I looked up eagerly.

"Stay out of the way."

15

Just as the detective had predicted, Sheriff Langley was waiting for us at the campground office as we pulled up minutes later. His arms were crossed, his expression even more so.

Swallowing, I pouted a little about being left out. I suppose I had invited myself along, but… it still stung.

The detective parked the SUV and we hopped out, congregating in front of the sheriff like some sort of super-hero squad, here to defeat evil and ensure justice for all. And the detective didn't waste any time.

"Langley." He nodded in hello, then turned to Alex. "Head on inside, son," he said, pointing to the office.

Before Langley could even argue, Alex was gone. I stayed put, half in awe, half unsure of how things were going to play out after this. I'd seen Detective Valdez work before. I knew he was good at what he did, but I'd never been on his side, never had his trust enough for him to involve me. To be honest, I wanted to soak it up.

"I'm going to need those files on James Mercer's death." Alex's dad squared his shoulders.

The sheriff set his jaw.

"You did bring them, correct?"

Langley's eyes were masked by dark sunglasses, but from the red tint creeping across his face, it was easy enough to see he was glaring, seething really. "I brought them," he said through gritted teeth, then pivoted and stalked over to his car, motioning for us to follow.

With a yank of the door to open and a slam to shut it, the sheriff proffered a file toward the detective. If it had been me, I would have snatched it from the man's hand triumphantly, rubbing it in, but Detective Valdez took it gently and began flipping through its contents.

"Throat cut... brake lines cut..." he read, then looked up. "No weapon has been recovered yet?"

The sheriff recrossed his arms and shook his head.

Detective Valdez returned his attention to the file. "And what of this journal found under the truck?"

"Nothing much, just notes and stuff." I could feel the sheriff's eyes lock on the detective through his tinted lenses.

I suppressed a gasp. Nothing important? What was wrong with him? That journal outlined the existence of an illegal fraternity, wrought with dysfunction and very possibly the reason James was dead and Matt was in the hospital. I wanted to call him on his lie.

But I kept it all to myself, because I was supposed to stay out of the way. Plus, the one thing more interesting than him lying was *why*.

Alex appeared in that moment, a few copies clutched in his hands. He came straight at us. Looking up, Detective Valdez noticed Alex, too. Snapping at me and his son, he pointed us over to a nearby picnic table.

"We'll let you know if we have any questions," the detective told Langley.

Once seated at the table, he spread out the papers in the file while Alex leafed through the camping registry. I stood, refraining from sitting next to Alex as that might look like I was getting involved. But I couldn't help leaning down and letting Alex know the latest development.

"The sheriff lied about the journal," I whispered, moving my mouth as little as possible in case Langley was secretly a lip reader.

Alex blinked. "Really?" He looked over at Langley who turned to walk inside the rangers' office.

Free to speak now that the sheriff was gone, I dipped my chin once. "Said it wasn't important. I know you guys have this whole *Jaws* theory where you think Langley could be downplaying this whole murder thing to preserve the last few weeks of camping season. I have a different idea." I leaned in close. "You guys ever read the book, *The Killer Inside Me* by Jim Thompson?" When they both shook their heads, I continued. "Well, it's about a small-town sheriff who is actually a serial killer. And, while your *Jaws* theory was cute, I'm thinking we could be dealing with a slash-happy sheriff."

Both cops, the men didn't seem as accepting of my theory.

"Pepper, accusing a cop of obstructing justice is one thing." Alex cringed.

"A very serious something," Detective Valdez said.

"But saying he is the one going around slashing people's throats and beating twenty-somethings to a pulp on the street is…"

"Not going to be something we consider unless more evidence points us in that direction," the detective finished for his son.

I put my hands up. "Okay, I'm not trying to undo the fabric of your entire career. It was just a thought."

The guys went back to looking through the papers and I turned the other way, glancing around the quiet camp-ground, pretending my job was to be on the lookout for the sheriff. When he didn't come out after a few minutes, I got bored and pivoted so I could look the other direction... which just happened to give me a perfect view of the registry Alex was looking through.

Glancing over his shoulder, I scanned the names, telling myself I was just searching for my own among the list of Friday campers. But then I came across a name I knew, one that definitely wasn't mine.

Gregory Wilford.

I sucked in a quick breath.

"What?" Alex asked, looking over his shoulder.

I scrunched my forehead together, remembering I was supposed to be staying out of the way. "Uh—nothing—I..." Faking a yawn, I took a few steps away from the table. "I'm going to walk around a little while you guys finish looking over all of that."

Alex eyed me for a few moments. "Okay, stay close. We won't be too much longer."

Detective Valdez looked up from his own papers and gave me a nod.

"Take your time." I waved a don't-worry-about-little-ol'-me hand in their direction as I pivoted and headed away.

Heat raced to my cheeks as I walked. That name sat like a lump in my gut. Gregory Wilford was the dean of students at NWU. My parents knew him. In fact, he'd been one of my dad's best friends back when they were in college and for years after. But when I was in high school, Dad and Gregory had some sort of falling out and I hadn't seen anyone from his family since.

I kept walking as my mind worked through the surprise of seeing his name there. But as my sandals crunched rhythmically along the path, my anxious stomach settled. NWU was only an hour away from this campground. It wasn't unlikely that members of the faculty would come here to vacation. In fact, Silver Falls was a favorite camp spot among the people of Pine Crest.

Which meant that just because I had recognized the man's name didn't mean he had anything to do with this whole debacle. The devil's advocate part of my brain chose that moment to remind me about the disagreement with a dean at NWU James had written about in his journal.

Gregory was a dean at NWU, and he'd been staying here that night.

A light breeze flowed around me, brushing back my hair and cooling my worry-warmed cheeks. I let out a chuckle and shook my head. No. There was no way. I didn't know what went on between Dr. Wilford and my father, but he was a good man. Plus, he had at least four inches of height on James, so he couldn't have been the killer in the first place.

Settled, I stopped walking. The campground was gone. I was surrounded by the creaking of tall trees, wind-rustled leaves, and the occasional, far-off birds calling to one another. My father's voice, deep and steady as it always became when he was reading to me, drifted into the silence of the forest. It was a line from Thoreau's diary.

"'The question is not what you look at, but what you see.' Isn't that the truth, Peps?" A boyish grin conquered his features as he glanced around the wild, sunlight catching in the red highlights in his hair.

I pulled in another deep breath of forest air and kept walking forward, trying to really *see* the beauty surrounding me.

I marveled at the lush green mosses and ferns that encroached upon my trail; even in this heat they grew abundantly in the shade of the pines and leafy maples. I listened to the hum of the mountain range in the distance, the whistle of the nearby valley, and the soft buzz of a million summer bugs.

There were rhododendrons of every color, some short, leafy, and pink, others tall as small trees with their winding, woody branches and white buds. A large boulder sat next to a nearby hill, settled now after tumbling down from higher up the mountain who knows when. There were fir trees standing so tall they swayed and creaked as if made woozy by their own height. Two madrona trees twisted together until their trunks melded into one. To my left there stood the hollow trunk of a giant which had long ago fallen, roots upended, like a hand emerging from the earth.

My feet crunched to a halt.

"It's not what you look at, but what you see," I murmured to myself as I squinted at the two boulders. Two. Nestled near the two twisting madronas. Higher up, their papery bark peeled in long curls, revealing new, green life beneath. But low, near the ground, their old trunks were gnarled and split. Of the larger knots, there were two which opened like holes into the tree.

They drew me in, pulled me nearer. Dad would've appreciated something like this. "Two boulders by two trees with two knots. Two, two, and two. Thoreau stayed in his cabin on Walden pond for two years, two months, and two days," Dad would've pointed out, and I would've marveled at his knowledge. We could spend hours out here reading quotes and looking for patterns just like this.

A smile pulling on my lips, I glanced behind me and froze, all of the happiness I'd felt in that moment drained out of me. My heartbeat ratcheted up as I realized I was standing just outside the clearing, hidden by the tall rhodies, where Hammy had led us to James's body. Spinning back toward the two trees in front of me, I saw them with new eyes. I wasn't the only one who'd been out here who knew a thing or two about Thoreau.

Had James noticed the same pattern I had? Was it possible he'd been out here in this specific clearing for a reason?

Excitement traded places with my fear momentarily as I stepped forward. Maybe James had hidden a clue, something that I could help us narrow down his killer. Sticking with my Thoreau theme, I skipped the first knot in the twisted trees and went straight for the second. A primal warning told me not to stick my hand into the dark crevice, so I pulled out my phone and clicked on the flashlight. Scooting a little closer, I was able to shine the light into the knot.

And that's when the light glinted off something metallic. My throat felt like it had dried up. Okay, so maybe it wasn't James who had left something behind, but someone else entirely.

Using the bottom of my T-shirt to cover my hand, I leaned in close and reached inside. My cotton-covered fingers closed around something. I pulled it out, stepping back, and my eyes widened at the knife swinging in front of me.

I'd managed to grab the blunt edge of the probably-four-inch hunting knife and I pinched my fingers tighter, hoping I wasn't compromising any fingerprints possibly remaining on any of the surfaces.

Still clutching my phone with my left hand, I moved to call Alex. Before I even had a chance to turn off the flashlight, however, I heard someone clear their throat behind me.

Jumping and spinning in one not-so-fluid motion, I let go of the knife in my surprise. Stepping back so I didn't impale a toe, the knife hit the forest floor with a heavy thud. My attention didn't stay on the potential murder weapon too long, however, because I was too interested—and horrified—in who was standing in front of me.

Sheriff Langley stood near the clearing, arms crossed, a twisted smile marring his already unpleasant face. "Whatever you do, do not pick that up."

16

The sheriff inched closer, reaching his hand forward. A bird squawked in the distance, making me jump. Langley was only about ten feet away at that point and I knew deep in my gut that I could not let him get his hands on this knife.

So as he continued to inch toward me, I began to sink into a squat.

He paused. There was a flicker of something like hatred in his eyes, but he quickly masked it with another fake smile. "You do *not* know who you're messing with, missy."

Missy? Anger flared in my chest. Eyes locked on him, I kept squatting lower, not giving him the grace of a response.

He began to move faster, so I abandoned my attempt to pick up the knife—what was I going to do anyway, grab it and run through the woods?—and stamped my foot down on the handle just as he lunged forward.

"Pepper?" Alex's voice rang through the quiet forest.

I froze and so did the sheriff. My sandaled foot pinned the knife down, but Langley's fingers were only inches away.

"Alex!" I yelled, narrowing my gaze at the sheriff in triumph.

Langley grumbled something and then moved to stand, brushing the pine needles and dirt off his uniform.

Hearing footsteps growing closer, I kept an eye on the sheriff, yelling, "Over he—!" But my voice cut out as I watched the sheriff's short sleeve slide up higher on his bicep from the motion of dusting himself off. Under the tan fabric was something I recognized immediately.

A tattoo of three As in a shape like the top of a star. Just like in James's journal. Just like in my dad's book. Eyes wide, I thought back to Dylan saying past members of the fraternity seemed to be the most upset about James's plan to move the organization.

The surprise of seeing the TriAlpha's symbol on the sheriff's arm was like swallowing too big a bite of oatmeal all at once. I couldn't speak, swallow, barely breathe.

Could I have been right? Could the sheriff really have been the one to kill James? He was just the right height, after all. The man didn't seem to notice that I'd seen, however, continuing to pat the dirt off his shins as Alex appeared around the group of rhodies. Sweat beaded on his forehead and his eyes were wild as he looked me up and down.

"You okay?" he asked, jogging over and quickly eyeing the sheriff who'd stepped a few feet back.

Gulping, I nodded.

"Dad, they're over here," he called over his shoulder.

I heard more footsteps crunch down the path. Alex turned back to me, his forehead creasing in worry as he took in my probably pale, shocked expression.

"You sure?"

Between the way my heart was trying to pound through

my chest and the yelled exclamations crashing through my brain, I couldn't put any words together. Instead, I just pointed down at the knife I still had pinned under my sandal. Dirt and pine needles had kicked up in our struggle and it was slightly buried. But I could tell from the way the muscles in Alex's jaw tightened that he knew what he was looking at.

He stepped toward the sheriff, pushing back his shoulders. "What was going on here?"

The sheriff pointed straight at me and yelled, "Ask the one compromising *my* evidence!"

Detective Valdez skidded to a stop in the clearing just as the sheriff finished shouting. The detective's eyebrows rose up and he looked to me.

Shaking my head, I finally found my voice. "That's not true. I found the knife and just as I was about to call you he lunged at me and tried to take it."

Kneeling next to me, Alex gently lifted my foot off the knife. He looked to his dad. "You have an evidence bag on you?"

"No, but I have a glove. It'll have to do until we can get this back to the car." The detective stepped forward, pulling a plastic glove from his pocket.

Just as he was about to pull the glove over his fingers, the sheriff cleared his throat. "Actually, I'll be taking the knife," he said, voice cold and calculated. "So you can give *me* the glove." He held out his hand.

Detective Valdez raised an eyebrow. "I thought we established that this was now——"

"We established *my* victim's friend was killed with a knife, not yours. This knife is the murder weapon in my case, which I very much doubt is even linked with yours."

He snapped his fingers and then curled them in and out, gesturing again for the glove.

"Sheriff…" the detective said; the word was a low growl in his throat.

"I humored you enough by letting you come out here. I can see now that I shouldn't have let it happen. Hand over my evidence, Detective." The sheriff stepped forward again. "Or I will make you regret it."

Detective Valdez exhaled audibly. In contrast, I held my breath, waiting for the police drama movie-style, stand-off about to happen, complete with a rousing speech to put this crooked sheriff in his place.

My mouth dropped open as the man I'd been counting on handed over the glove. The sheriff slipped it on and knelt quickly to grab the evidence from the ground in front of me. Our evidence.

"But… you can't—he didn't—" My wild eyes shifted between the two lawmen.

The detective held up his hand to stop me. "It's okay, Miss Brooks. He's right."

"He also never would've found the knife if it wasn't for me." Exasperation raised the tone and pitch of my voice until I was almost yelling.

I was about to say something about his tattoo when a gentle hand landed on my shoulder. I glanced over to see Alex standing beside me. His dark eyes implored me to listen. *Alex too?* My shoulders slumped under the weight of his insistence and my chin dipped toward my chest.

"Okay," I mumbled.

On the walk back to the campground, Alex came up beside me a few minutes in and wrapped an arm around my waist, pulling me close while we walked. The sheriff and

Alex's dad were a good ten feet in front of us, but I slowed my pace, making Alex drop back a little more with me.

"He's one of them," I whispered, eyebrows setting in a hard line on my forehead. "He has the TriAlpha symbol tattooed on his arm."

Alex swallowed, his Adam's apple bobbing. He watched the sheriff for a moment, then said, "You think he might be trying to protect someone in the group? I thought we'd decided it wasn't likely it was one of the frat guys."

"Maybe not a *current* member of the frat. But what about an alumnus?" I cocked an eyebrow at him. "Remember what Dylan said about past members of the frat being angrier than the active ones? What if the sheriff killed James, but Kevin is convinced it was Matt and he beat him up to get back at him?"

"Pepper." Alex sighed. "We're not back to this, are we? A sheriff did not slit a college kid's throat in the middle of the woods just to stop him from moving his old frat to another university."

Tipping my head onto his shoulder, I wrinkled my nose. The man had a point. "I know, but he's one of them. Doesn't that mean something?" Thoughts and worries about my dad flooded the sentiment behind my question, unbeknownst to Alex.

"Not necessarily." He shrugged.

I looked up at him. "Really?" I knew I'd done a bad job of concealing my eagerness when Alex glanced down.

"What's up with you?" he asked, stopping and facing me. His fingers intertwined with mine. "Everything okay?"

Truth was... no, it wasn't. Ever since I found that symbol in Dad's book, I had a gnawing worry in my gut. And the terrible feeling was only made worse by the knowledge I was keeping it from Alex. I breathed out my reservations in a whoosh, knowing I could remedy at least one of the things bothering me.

"Remember when we were looking through the boxes of my dad's books?"

Alex nodded. "And you went all weird after you found his copy of *Civil Disobedience*."

I shook my head and laughed. "And here I thought I'd covered it up so well. That's what I get for dating a cop, huh?"

He leaned forward to kiss me. "I was trying to give you space with it. Wanted you to tell me when you were ready."

"I think my dad was in the TriAlphas, too," I said, my words almost a whisper.

Alex's face contorted into a scowl. "What? Why?"

"When I was paging through his copy of *Civil Disobedience*, I saw he'd sketched the three As under his name on the title page." I grimaced. The words burned like stomach acid in my throat.

He pulled in a deep breath, then let it go, shaking his head. "Well, I have to admit I didn't see that coming, but…" He shrugged. "I still don't think it automatically means something bad about him."

"How?" I tried to keep my voice from becoming shrill in my frustration. "Alex, these are terrible people who are not only breaking the law, but seem to have a complete disregard for life. How is it *not* absolutely devastating that my dad was a part of an organization like this?"

Alex's hands moved to cup my face. "Peps, you have to trust that you knew your dad, that the man you loved wouldn't have done something like this." He dropped his hands to rest on my shoulders. "When my mom was shot…" He cleared his throat. "She—there were quite a few people who commented on her obituary, saying pretty awful things.

They hid behind their anonymous online profiles and said she deserved to die because she was a dirty cop who got involved where she shouldn't have. Dad and I—" His voice cut out, but he tried again. "We had to remember who she was, and we couldn't let anything they said diminish it. You have to do the same thing, now."

Blinking back tears, I took a deep breath as Alex's face tightened from the memory. Then I lunged forward and wrapped my arms around his stomach, squeezing tight while I buried my face into his chest.

"I'm so sorry you had to deal with that." My words were muffled by his T-shirt, which only made them feel even more insufficient.

He slipped his arms behind me and held me, resting his chin on the top of my head. "I'm not quite sure what I would've done without my dad to help me get through. Do you think talking with your mom would help? She might know something you don't about the whole situation. Might help clear things up."

Pressing my lips together, I said, "Yeah. I should talk with her. I just got so mad at her last time we were there…"

Regret rose in my throat, making me feel too hot. I'm sure none of this was easy for Mom either, but she'd always been the kind to compartmentalize her feelings and deal with life first. Maggie had taken after her, still able to seem like she was keeping it together even when things were falling apart. Dad and I were the emotional, expressive ones. We quoted literature and cried over poetry and *felt* every single feeling. And while our way was decidedly messier, I didn't envy the silent, internal rollercoaster Mom must be experiencing with Duncan moving in.

Pulling away from Alex, I made a resolution to be more

gentle with my mother, and to talk with her about this whole TriAlpha thing.

"Come on. Let's go catch up." Alex kept an arm around me as we pointed ourselves back toward the campground and the two men we could no longer see.

Alex's father was waiting in the SUV when we arrived. The sheriff's cruiser was nowhere to be seen. Once we were inside, the detective donned his sunglasses and started the car.

"You two okay?" he asked as he pulled out of the campground parking lot.

Alex looked back at me.

"Yeah," I said. "Sheriff Langley is in the fraternity, though, or was."

"Ah," he said, gracefully leaving off the, "So that's why you were acting so crazy" part of his sentence.

"And while I'll concede there's not a whole lot of evidence to support him as a viable suspect, I do think he may be committing perjury to keep this whole thing under wraps."

The detective's sunglasses made it difficult to tell if he was watching me in the rearview mirror or if his eyes were remaining on the road.

"Not covering up for the sake of tourism, but loyalty to a fraternity. Now that makes much more sense. I apologize for the frustration we caused you back there, Pepper. Our showing up here was tenuous at best, but once the sheriff began to call me on it, I had no choice but to concede. He was right. The evidence is linked to his case, not mine. Until we can prove whether or not the two attacks are linked, we're not going to get that knife."

"Makes sense." Now that I had a little time removed from the situation, I could see how I had overreacted.

"Rest assured I will check up on the evidence, make sure it's submitted correctly. I will also look into the journal. If the sheriff is committing perjury, I will make sure he's dealt with accordingly."

I smiled. "Thank you. I'm sorry I was pushy. Sometimes I have a hard time with things not going how I think they should. But 'A man is rich in proportion to the number of things which he can afford to let alone,' right?"

Alex let out a little groan, but the detective dipped his head in a nod. "I agree, but with one caveat: only until he knows which things he cannot afford to let alone any longer." He paused for a moment. "Who said that?"

"Who else?" Alex chimed in.

"Thoreau," I answered, ignoring Alex. "It was one of my dad's favorite quotes."

In the mirror, the detective's lips tightened into a thin line. "Your father sounds like he was a wise man."

Letting go of the sick feeling of betrayal eating away at me ever since I'd found the symbol in his book, I let myself heed Alex's advice. "He was." A full smile spread across my face. "I miss him every single day, as I'm sure you know." My words were quiet, but they felt all too big even for the large interior of the SUV.

Alex nodded.

But the detective pulled his sunglasses off, setting them on top of his head before taking his eyes off the road to glance back at me. He could've just as easily met my eyes through the mirror, but I guess this was something he felt deserved actual eye contact.

"I still hear her singing sometimes in the morning," he said after a few moments. "She used to love singing as she got ready in the morning."

I could see Alex glance over at his father, his mouth parted in surprise.

"Different state, different house, heck... different bathroom, but I can still hear that sweet voice of hers floating through the bedroom, bouncing off the tiles."

"What a Wonderful World," Alex said, the words almost a hum they were surrounded by so much warmth.

"It was her favorite," Alex's father said.

And then the two of them began to hum the melody together, melting what was left of my broken heart.

We spent the rest of the drive sharing stories, them about Julie and me about Jackson, my father. As we pulled into Pine Crest, I knew I needed to talk with my mother.

"Alex, I might take a raincheck on hanging out more today."

"No problem," he said, unsurprised, as if he already knew what I was going to say.

"Would you mind dropping me off at my mom's office instead of my apartment, then?"

"Sure thing," the detective said.

Alex directed him there and before I knew it—or was ready for it—we were pulling up in front of my mother's firm situated in the heart of downtown.

I paused before getting out. "Thank you so much for bringing me along, Detective Valdez."

He turned to face me. "Thank you for finding the murder weapon." He winked. "I can honestly say we wouldn't have been able to do that without your literary intuition."

I ducked my head in a little bow, then reached forward to squeeze Alex's shoulder in a goodbye.

"Oh, and Pepper..." the detective said as I was sliding

out of my seat. When I looked back, he added, "Call me, Mateo. Okay?"

Stunned, I could only nod and close the door. Then I jogged the rest of the way to my mother's office building. I didn't know what I would learn about my dad when I entered, but one thing was for certain, I was glad Detective Valdez—Mateo—had ruined our Pepper and Alex day.

17

Unfortunately, my mother couldn't see me, having just connected with what was going to be a *long* conference call, according to her assistant. So I wandered the streets of downtown for a little bit, poking into my favorite thrift shop, Second Pantses, to see if she'd gotten in anything new.

It wasn't until I was trying on a particularly flowy scarf that I remembered my mother might not be the only one who knew my father well enough to give me information about his alleged fraternity involvement.

After hanging the scarf back on its hanger, I walked out into the summer sunshine and set a course for the English building on campus, only stopping by the bookshop briefly to pick up Dad's copy of *Civil Disobedience*.

The new quarter wouldn't begin until tomorrow, but I knew my favorite professor would be in her office, preparing an amazing lecture for the knowledge-hungry students about to file into her classroom.

The reality that I was quite possibly headed toward some answers about my father should've made me breathe in deep, relieved lungfuls of mountain air. But all I could do as I walked through campus was think about that damn symbol. When I'd seen it embroidered onto James's sleeve, I thought I'd recognized it from around the university, but now it seemed just as possible I'd seen it at home. And as much as I tried to hold tight to Alex's advice about knowing my dad's true character, I couldn't help but feel betrayed, led astray.

I kept up my pace and before I knew it, arrived at the pod which currently housed Professor Ferguson's office—and used to house my father's. Keeping my eyes forward, I walked straight.

"Oh!" She jumped when I stepped inside and knocked on the door frame. "Hello, Pepper. What can I do for you?" the older woman asked, blinking up at me through her thick, red-rimmed glasses. "You do remember classes don't begin until tomorrow, right?" She tittered at her joke and set down the paper she'd been looking over. "How is that bookstore of yours doing, my dear?"

Unready for the amount of questions she would have for me, I took a second to collect myself. "The bookstore is great," I said, finally. "I'm taking a few days off, things were getting a little stressful juggling that and my grad classes, so…" I blinked.

"Yes, yes, I bet." Fergie nodded. "I'm glad you've been able to take a much-needed respite."

Little did Fergie know that my "vacation" had been anything but restful. Since we'd found James's body, I'd actually been wishing for the albeit hectic, but comfortable, routine of a full class schedule and managing my bookstore. But I wasn't here to commiserate with Professor Ferguson about my stressful weekend, I was here for some answers.

"Fergie," I said, pulling out the Thoreau volume from

my bag. "I have something really important to ask you about my father."

Her face dropped and paled in color until it was apparent that any rosiness in her cheeks was due only to her bright pink blush. She wrung her hands together on top of the desk.

"Oh dear, I knew this day would come. But I suppose it's best to just rip it off, all at once, like a Band-Aid." She exhaled quickly.

My heart pounded as I waited. This was it, I could feel it.

Fergie nodded. "I'm afraid that your fears are, unfortunately, justified. Your father *was* an unapologetic fan of Thoreau." She burst into a loud laugh, causing me to jump out of surprise. "His interest in Shakespeare and Dickens were the only things which saved his literary soul, if you ask me."

"Bu—hi—" I sputtered out pieces of words, caught off guard by Fergie's humor.

All of a sudden, she seemed to recognize the pain etched onto my face and her laughter ceased. "Pepper, tell me you haven't gone over to the disobedient side, too?" She widened her eyes in mock horror.

Every fiber of the woman sitting in front of me had a flair for the dramatic. From her bright blue eyeshadow—applied liberally, full lid—to her wispy, blond combover and her long, draped clothing made her look like she was always on her way to some theatrical premier. The odd part was that she appreciated humor almost more than all of the drama, so sometimes it was easy to get caught off guard by her looking on the bright side.

Through all of my anticipation and anxiety, a laugh found a way, bubbling up and out of me. Giggling for a few moments, I wiped the smile off my face, slumping into the armchair in the corner of her office.

"No, Fergie. It's something serious, really." Flipping to the title page of the book, I handed it over to her, bridging the space in between her desk and the chair I occupied.

She clasped the book in her bony fingers and furrowed her brow. Readjusting her glasses, she peered at the page.

"Have you ever heard of a fraternity called Alpha Alpha Alpha?" They call themselves the TriAlphas."

Fergie pursed her lips. "Not very original, if you ask me. The whole Greek alphabet at their fingertips and they simply repeated the first letter three times?" She scoffed, but then seemed to remember she was supposed to be answering my question instead of hers. "Oh, um… no dear. I can't say I have. But I never got into all of that Greek business, something I was especially grateful for when we lost those poor boys that year."

"I know. And up until the other day, I would've said my father felt the same way, but look." I pointed, refocusing her attention. "That's the symbol for the fraternity, in his book."

"Well…" she scratched her long fingernails along her forehead. "It does seem to allude to a level of ownership, but I couldn't say for sure, dear."

I exhaled my hopes of Fergie knowing anything concrete which might help me.

"Have you talked with your mother about this?" she asked, glancing up from the book.

"I tried, but she's busy. I don't know. I guess I thought since you two were close, and since you knew him as a student *and* a fellow professor, you might be able to shed some light on things."

Something I said must've sparked something in the old

woman, because her penciled-in eyebrows shot up, along with a single bony finger.

"Pepper, dear. I may be unable to help you, yes, but I do remember your father and Dr. Wilford were very close during those years. If your mother is unable to help you with the information you seek, it's possible Gregory might."

Gregory Wilford. The name slipped back into my mind so easily since I'd just looked at it mere hours earlier. My toes scrunched up in my sandals as I realized the connection.

"Thanks, Fergie." I shot out of the chair and gave her a wave. "See you tomorrow!"

"I hope you're ready for Advanced Poetry Workshop, Pepper dear. I know *iamb!*" She called the terrible poetry pun after me making me smile even in my haste.

My feet flew over the tiled halls of the English building, then over the concrete walkways of campus, and finally over the industrial carpet of The Student Services Office. I probably should've gone to see if my mother was done with her meeting first or maybe called Alex to tell him what I was about to do, but I was too excited about the prospect of finally learning the truth about my dad, that I couldn't stop.

Gregory having been at the campground that night definitely made him a suspect, but this was my dad's old friend. I'd known him since I was a baby, back in the old days we'd even had dinner over at his house a few times. Plus I knew for a fact he was over six foot, so he sure didn't sound like he fit the murderer's profile.

His secretary showed me back, only pausing briefly when I told her I didn't have an appointment. I insisted it was important I see him now, and her smile widened into that fake, customer service range, eyes flicking up and down uncomfortably while she called into his office to see if he was free. Luckily, he agreed to see me, and in I went.

Gregory Wilford wore a big grin as I entered. He stood and came at me from around the desk, hand outstretched, body looming over me. Okay, maybe he was even taller than I'd remembered. The guy was almost as tall as Nate. Definitely not the throat slasher, then.

"Pepper Brooks! Gosh, it's great to see you! What has it been, years?" His voice boomed around his office. I got the feeling his secretary could hear every word through the thick wooden door.

"Three, just about." My gaze fell to the floor, along with my stomach. The last time I'd seen him was at my father's funeral.

Gregory shook his head, running his hand across his chin. "Right. Sorry. I still can't believe it sometimes."

I gave him a quick smile to show him it was okay, that I felt the same way. "Dr. Wilford, there's something I need to ask you."

"Sure, sure. Have a seat." He gestured to the chair across from his desk and then made his way back around to his side, sitting at the same time I sunk into the worn leather seat. "What's up?"

Swallowing, I took a quick moment to gather my thoughts. "You and my father spent a lot of time together during college, right?"

"We were roommates our first year on campus, actually."

"Right." I'd remembered Dad saying something about that once. "Can you tell me about his involvement in the fraternity called the TriAlphas?"

Gregory's jaw tightened. "Sorry, but I've never heard of it."

"Oh. I just thought…" The leather chair squeaked as I shifted uncomfortably. I turned my attention downward so he might not see the disappointment on my face. Discomfort filled the room, taking up the space left behind from his booming voice. I babbled, trying to create some noise in the awkward silence. "I stumbled on something of his and—never mind, just because he wrote a symbol in a book doesn't mean he was a part of the fraternity. And just because some of its members are crooked doesn't mean he was, too. We were at the campground at Silver Falls this weekend, just like you, and I don't know if you heard yet, but—"

"How do you know I was at Silver Falls?" Gregory asked, pulling my attention back up to his face.

Heat flooded my cheeks. "Oh, I—there was—my boyfriend is a cop. He's looking into the case. I may have glanced at the registration sign in at the campground."

Gregory's face darkened for a moment, like a cloud passing overhead. A chill skittered down my spine at the anger behind the look, and I wondered if maybe I was wrong to exclude the man so quickly from the suspect list. Whether or not he was keeping something from me about my father, he was definitely keeping some sort of secret and it didn't seem pleasant.

"You mentioned a case?" he asked, rubbing his face with his palm, looking very tired all of a sudden. "Are you talking about the kid that was killed?"

I nodded. The rangers had obviously filled in the campers as they were asking questions the other morning.

Gregory's eyes closed slowly, his face losing its rosy coloring. "They didn't say how he died, just asked if we'd seen anything."

"Someone slit his throat." I gritted my teeth, hating to be the bearer of such dismal news.

Oddly, Gregory's face softened at this news, as if he was relieved to hear it. My face hardened at the sight, and he must've noticed because he said, "Sorry, I'm not happy about that... per se. I'm just happy to hear it wasn't another overdose situation."

Taking a stab based on how oddly Dylan had acted when I'd brought the name up yesterday, I asked, "Like Ethan Emsworth?"

Gregory puffed out his cheeks. "Yes."

"Dr. Wilford, what do you know about Ethan's death?" I asked. I'd heard about it, of course, three years earlier. But it had happened right before my dad passed away and I was just trying to get by, catch up in my classes, so it hadn't really made my radar.

Whatever had been holding Gregory back seemed to snap at the mention of Ethan. His body slumped forward slightly, making his tall frame shrink behind the desk.

"I know the poor boy deserved better. His family deserved better."

"Better than what?"

Gregory sighed, blue eyes filled with pain as he looked at me. "Pepper, your dad and I..." He swallowed, then dropped his gaze to the floor. "You were right, Jackson." The statement was a whisper.

Hearing my dad's name devastated me into stunned silence. What did he have to do with Ethan Emsworth's death?

The floor creaked outside, and the sound of a cupboard shutting reverberated through the room. I sucked in a worried breath.

"I can't do this anymore," Gregory said after a moment.

"You deserve to know the truth. It's the least I can do since the last thing I did for your father was let him down."

My heart pounded, loud and overwhelming in my ears as he opened his lower desk drawer and fumbled around for a moment. After locating what he was looking for, he pulled it out, facing it toward me. I laid my eyes on the TriAlpha symbol again. This time it was printed on a swatch of fabric about the size of a notebook.

"I lied earlier. I have heard of the fraternity. In fact, your father and I were the ones who created it."

18

It felt as if Gregory's words materialized into a fist and landed right into my stomach, completely knocking the wind out of me.

"What?" I wheezed as I sank deeper into the leather office chair.

His face wrinkled in concern. "I'm sorry. I don't know how you found out about it or what you've heard, but you have to believe me, the TriAlphas are not the same now as they were when we started all of those years ago."

I felt like my throat was raw with questions. "What was it like?" I asked, finally settling on one of the many swimming through my mind.

Gregory's lips quirked up in a quiet nostalgia. "We were out to change the world, for the better." His eyes, which had been wandering off again, locked onto mine. "One night during our freshman year, your father and I were up late and we got to talking about Thoreau, about *Walden*, but mostly about *Civil Disobedience*. Our young minds couldn't seem to fathom the unfair world we were preparing ourselves to be a part of. We felt caged in by rules, misunderstood by those in charge, and disenchanted with the idea of becoming just another cog in a failed machine.

"So we thought up the fraternity, a way we could watch out for each other, a way we could get around at least some of the imbalance we saw in the world, like the clever loon Thoreau writes about, slipping just out of reach. It would be a brotherhood unlike any other. We would vow to always support our members, to always recognize the symbol of the TriAlphas, and to help whenever there was a need."

I listened, trying to picture my father as an impressionable eighteen-year-old who just wanted to make the world a better place.

"We'd only just started gaining steam when there were those deaths during rush week and the university decided to ban anything to do with the Greek system. But we weren't like the others. We were all about supporting our fellow man. We didn't even rush at the same time, picking spring when life was given a new start instead of fall like all the rest. And we weren't ready to let all of that go just because the others had screwed things up.

"So we went underground. Disobedience is the true foundation of liberty, after all. We only invited a select few to rush each spring, we picked only the best of character and the brightest of minds. And because your dad and I both stayed around after graduation, we continued on as president and vice president for a few years. Eventually, though, our lives got a little more hectic; we both married, started having kids, and we handed the reigns over to someone else, someone we trusted implicitly.

"But over the years, our ideals were slowly lost, as it goes when something is copied many times over. The brotherhood became more like a true fraternity and the new presidents started to care more about the elite nature of being a secret fraternity. They began to take advantage of the knowledge that the alumnus would have their back, get them out of sticky situations, and because they could, they began to get into stickier and stickier situations.

Gregory shook his head. "I convinced campus security to look the other way when they caught them partying, I changed a member's grades when they got behind in their coursework and started to fail classes. I'm not proud of any of it." Gregory locked eyes with me. "And your father hated it. Once he realized the whole thing was going downhill, he stopped coming to their rescue, told me I needed to cut ties too; it wasn't what we'd created any more. But I was already in too deep. The things I'd done could be used as blackmail, easily be grounds for me losing my position.

"James was the first president to bring hazing into rush week. We tried to put a stop to it, but he wouldn't listen, said we were old and washed up, what did we know? Ethan Emsworth was in the first batch of pledges to be put through what James liked to call, Civil Obedience. He created a trivia game about Thoreau and for every question they got wrong, pledges had to take a shot." Gregory sighed. "There were a hundred questions, so even if they only missed a few, it's a lot of shots.

"Ethan missed thirteen."

"And you helped cover it up." My voice sounded small after so much of Gregory's consuming the small space of his office.

He met my gaze, then looked down. "I did. Your father was absolutely furious with me. He told me I'd become just like the striped snake, oblivious to what was really going on around me." Dr. Wilford pinched the bridge of his nose with his thumb and pointer finger. "I told him if he told anyone about what we'd done, I would make sure everyone found out it was he who started it, and I would ruin his career. It was the last thing I said to him. He had his heart attack a week later."

Gregory swallowed, then swiped at the corners of his eyes.

"I don't even care if I get fired anymore. Living with this burden for so many years has been eating away at me. Just like Jackson told me I should, I need to finally accept the consequences for my actions, once and for all. It's the least I can do for him since the stress from our fight, from the position I put him in, could've been what brought on his heart attack."

In that moment, my own heart felt like it was simultaneously breaking and mending. Watching this man's guilt over his actions hurt, especially since he'd obviously cared about my father. But I couldn't help the lightness which came over me at the news that, not only had my father not been behind the ugly side of the fraternity, but also that he'd been against hiding what happened to Ethan.

I got up. Maneuvering around the desk, I wrapped my arms around his broad shoulders in a sympathetic side-hug.

"We did the same thing—a lot, at first," I said, pulling away. "We blamed ourselves for what we didn't see, what we could've done. But the doctors assured us it was a mix of a lot of factors. He wasn't overweight and he didn't seem particularly stressed at any given time. He definitely should've gone in for a physical every now and then, but…" I sighed. "We can't go back in time."

It was possible I needed to hear those words even more than Dr. Wilford, because as they left my mouth, I began to feel a bit of calm settle over me. After operating under a high level of paranoia and worry since finding the symbol in Dad's book, I began to let go.

"Thank you, Pepper." Gregory dipped his chin in appreciation as I moved to sit down again. "Your father was a good man and I miss him very much."

"Me too." Now that my emotional baggage was clearing, separating from the case, something from my conversation with Chloe came back to me. "You weren't in any kind of contact with James before he died, were you?" I asked.

Gregory grimaced for a moment before saying, "I was helping him with the plan to move the fraternity to Southern Washington University. I know a few of the professors and one of the deans down there and I thought maybe if I could get the TriAlphas away from here, I could get out of having to do their dirty work anymore." Suddenly, Gregory's expression fell. "Wait. You don't think our plan is what got James killed, do you?"

I shook my head. "I did at first, but then the vice president, Matt, was attacked, too. He's in the ICU, still hasn't woken up. He was completely against the move. He'd been my biggest suspect, up until he became a victim as well."

"Yes, I heard about Matt. You think the two incidents are related?" Gregory's brow furrowed.

Sighing, I said, "My gut tells me they are, but there's no proof, yet. They weren't attacked in the same way, of course, which doesn't help my theory."

"I guess we won't know for sure until Matt wakes up," Gregory said.

"If he wakes up," I added somberly, remembering how Alex had described his injuries.

Gregory rubbed his palms over his face and took a deep breath. "This whole thing became so much bigger, so much more complicated than Jackson or I could've ever predicted."

Narrowing my eyes, I got an idea. "So would you help me figure out how to clean it up, if you could?"

Dr. Wilford nodded. "Absolutely. Anything you need."

I leaned forward. "Tell me about Sheriff Jefferson Langley."

Gregory's face darkened. "Rushed about ten years ago when I was still involved with looking over pledges for them. He's a power-happy punk, that's all."

"Well, he's a punk with a lot of the evidence we need, and I think he might be hiding something."

Gregory pushed his shoulders back. "Got it. Let me make a few calls. I'll see what I can do."

I smiled, standing. "Anything you can get him to share with Detective Mateo Valdez at the Pine Crest Police Department, would be greatly appreciated."

"Anything else?" he asked.

Biting my lip, I thought about it. "I'm guessing you know all about Chloe French."

He dipped his chin. "The girl who wrote the blog earlier this year."

"And making her seem crazy so no one would take her seriously was yet another string you pulled to keep the TriAlphas a secret?"

He held his thumb and pointer finger up, only leaving a small space in between the two. "I only had to do a little on that one, she did the rest. She hid the fact that she and Dylan Oakes were an item."

I shuffled my feet on the carpet as I thought through what I'd just heard. "Why would that matter?"

"Discredits her story. Makes it seem like the only reason she believed him was because they were dating."

Blinking, I remembered how Chloe had gotten all weird when she'd told us about her and Dylan dating, adamant they'd gotten together because of the fallout from the article, not before it.

"That lie only came to light after her big mistake, though," Gregory said, thoughtfully.

"Big mistake?"

"I'm assuming she told you all about how the fraternity planted the failed drug test that got him kicked off the team?"

"Yep."

"They found traces of amphetamines in his urine. Chloe, sure Dylan hadn't been taking anything, must've looked up how long amphetamines can stay in the body." Gregory stopped, looking to me as if I might know the answer.

I shrugged.

"Forty-eight hours. She promptly went to the athletic department and told them she'd been with Dylan for the last forty-eight hours other than when he was in class and that there was no way he'd taken any drugs."

"Which he hadn't, right?"

"Correct, but at the same time Chloe was telling them about one alibi, Dylan was giving a completely different one to his coach."

Sighing, I shook my head.

"So even though Dylan was probably telling the truth, between this being his second offense—the alcohol overdose and then the failed drug test—and the confusion between his story and Chloe's, the coach couldn't take a chance on him."

My mind rewound back to Alex asking Dylan where he'd been that weekend. The way he'd paused, asked if we'd asked Chloe the same question, and then had shared that look with his roommate, it all screamed something was up.

"Pepper, is everything okay?" Dr. Wilford asked, leaning closer toward me.

"Uh—I—yeah… I just—that's interesting information. It just changes a lot."

"For the better, I hope."

Licking my lips, I shook my head. "I don't know yet. Thanks, Dr. Wilford." I waved and spun on my heel to leave.

"Be careful, Pepper. Please," Gregory called after me as I reached the door.

I smiled, nodded, and then pulled open the door. Once I'd jogged out of the student services building, I dug my phone out of my pocket then dialed Alex.

"Hey," he answered.

"I think Dylan's alibi is false," I blurted, settling on a nearby concrete bench. I eyed a couple walking by, but they didn't seem to notice me or what I'd said.

"Why?"

"Chloe's lied to protect him before, so what if she's covering for him again? Remember when he asked if we'd already talked to Chloe before he would give his alibi?"

"Yeah…" I could practically hear Alex putting it all together through the phone.

"And then he and Liam shared that look, as if they had an understanding? It was almost as if Dylan was silently asking Liam to go with whatever he said."

"Liam did seem to stumble on that alibi," Alex reasoned.

"Because Dylan's the murderer," I said, cutting through the silence Alex had left while he thought.

19

"He had the motive," I said, standing to pace outside student services, holding my phone close, so I didn't have to speak loudly for Alex to hear me. "They ruined his baseball career by getting him kicked off the team. He hated them."

"It would also explain why he not only went for James, but Matt as well," Alex added.

"Right. If we can prove that his alibi was false, would that be enough to bring him in for questioning?"

"Definitely. I think we need to pay him a visit, see if we can find out what he was really doing." There was a shuffle of noise on the other end and it sounded like Alex was on the move. "I'm coming to get you. Where are you at?"

I scanned the mostly empty walkways surrounding me. "On campus. North end."

"Got it. Meet me at the corner of Madrona and Main in five minutes. I'm going to call Dylan and see if he'll meet us and where."

Hanging up, I started walking north. A few minutes later, Alex pulled up in his truck, leaning over to push open the passenger door for me. I scooted inside and glanced over at him. His eyebrows were pulled tight over his dark eyes.

"What? He won't meet with us?" I asked.

"He will, but he wants us to come to his apartment."

I cringed. That didn't sound good.

Alex seemed to share my feelings, because he said, "If he has any idea we're onto him, this could be a trap."

My stomach flipped uncomfortably at the statement. "Well, we have each other. Two against one." I shrugged.

Alex laughed. "Or, you know, the fact that I'm carrying a gun."

I dipped my head to one side in concession. "That too."

Dylan's apartment was located on the opposite side of campus as mine, but it still only took us a few minutes to get there. I caught sight of Alex's gun holster, strapped onto his belt as he adjusted his shirt over it.

We walked up to the second floor, apartment six, in silence. I didn't know about Alex, but my mind was working all too fast, going through scenarios and questions and worries and fears to put a coherent sentence together.

Alex's knuckles rapping on the door kicked me out of my head. The door swung open and Dylan stood before us.

"Come on in." Stepping back, he made room for us to enter.

The smell of ramen noodles permeated the air of the sparsely decorated apartment. Not a huge surprise given two college guys lived here. There was a large television across from a faded couch in the small living room, dishes piled up in the sink, and what appeared to be two bedrooms from what little I could see through the opened doors.

"Uh... we don't have a table. Mind sitting here?" He pointed to a tall eating bar on the other side of the kitchen.

Scooting a few piles of books and paper aside, he made room for us, staying in the kitchen so we were facing him.

Alex and I climbed onto two tall bar stools while Dylan paced before us. I tucked my feet onto one of the chair rungs, resisting the urge to wiggle my foot as an outlet for my anxiety.

"So you're getting close, huh?" he asked, finally, looking up at us. "Was I right? It was Matt, wasn't it?"

My eyes narrowed as I studied Dylan. Did he really not know about Matt or was he just trying to fool us?

"He's one of the people we're watching," Alex said.

Dylan nodded. "Cool, cool. So what can I help you with?"

I wracked my brain for a way to broach the subject of Dylan's alibi without cluing him into the reason for our visit.

Beating me to it, Alex said, "Besides Matt, can you walk us through the guys who might've had reason to want James out of the picture.

The next few minutes felt like hours as Dylan went through every intricate detail of the inner workings of the frat. He remained adamant that Kevin was innocent, but had no trouble pointing the finger at the rest of the frat. My stomach flipped as he even brought up the dean of students holding meetings with James over the past few months.

"None of that matters, though, because Matt had to have been the one to do it," he said as he finished.

I almost let out a scoff of surprise. He was still pretending he didn't know what had happened to Matt? Did he really think we wouldn't know?

"You seem to know an awful lot about the fraternity for someone who didn't make it in." Alex crossed his arms, probably thinking just the same indignant questions I was.

Dylan's expression froze for a split second, but he recovered into a sly smile. "I pay attention… know what I'm looking at, or whatever Thoreau said."

The high-pitched laugh he let out after made me grit my teeth almost as much as the butchered quote. Doubt began to cloud my earlier certainty. Not only was that the poorest excuse for a quote I'd ever heard, but this guy sure didn't seem like the kind to notice the two, two, two pattern in the forest where the knife was hidden. Gregory had just told me Ethan overdosed because he missed thirteen of the Thoreau questions. If Dylan had been in danger of doing the same, wouldn't he have to miss almost as many?

Something wasn't adding up. I watched Dylan carefully. It was possible he was pretending not to be familiar with Thoreau to throw us off his trail.

Alex and Dylan continued to chat about all of the research Dylan did during rush week to learn so much, but I decided to take Dylan's own—albeit poorly worded—advice and pay attention to what was around me.

Besides the old plates and dirty pans littering the kitchen, there didn't seem to be much of anything I could use there. I turned my gaze to the papers littering the countertop next to the place Dylan had cleared off for me. It was difficult to appear as if I were still following the conversation while glancing down at the pile of bills and opened mail next to me. So much so, in fact, I felt the need to take a break or I was going to have some sort of dizzy spell.

"Can I use your bathroom?" I asked, interrupting the guys.

Dylan looked up at me, blinked. "Uh, yeah. Straight through there." He pointed to the room to our right.

I slid myself off the stool, then headed into Dylan's bedroom. It was fairly clean—actually, organized was a better word, the place had an interesting sweaty socks and body spray smell to it—with a few shirts piled on the bed and a stack of books tottering on the small desk. The door was open, so I couldn't exactly snoop, but I slowed my steps as I passed by his desk. There was a calendar pinned onto the wall. I squinted at it.

And my breath caught in my throat.

My heart hammered loudly in my ears as I stared at the same jagged handwriting from the journal we'd found under James's truck. Looking at the other papers pinned around it only confirmed my terrified suspicions. Flustered, I scrambled into the bathroom and realized it was a Jack and Jill bathroom just like at my apartment. I shut both doors then turned on the faucet, my fingers slipped clumsily on the chrome as I did so. The me reflected in the mirror was breathing heavily and wearing shifty, worried eyes.

I'd been wrong to assume the journal was James's just because it was under his truck. Suddenly everything made perfect sense. Dylan had been studying the fraternity, writing down everything he knew about in the months since he almost died of alcohol poisoning. He must've dropped the journal while he was cutting the brakes on James's truck that night. I thought back to the sneaking shadow we'd seen silhouetted in the fabric of our tent that night. It had been Dylan sneaking around.

But why would he leave that journal behind?

I remembered Detective Valdez talking about the traces of brake solvent in the wound on James's throat and it all became clear.

If Dylan had been trying to take out as many of the frat members as he could, cutting their brakes was a great way to do that. But what if he heard the fight between Matt and James, then heard James stumble off into the woods alone?

He had already stolen Matt's knife. The chance to meet his enemy face-to-face probably became too good to pass up.

Scooting out from under the truck in a hurry, Dylan must've dropped the journal, and I'd found it before he had a chance to come back.

Thinking about the journal, I remembered the section on internal and external cracks. It hadn't been James writing down the weaknesses in his own organization. It was Dylan trying to figure out how to break them, how to kill the people who'd wronged him and blame it on others. He'd been way too adamant it had to be Matt who'd killed James, after all.

And I'd played right into it. My heart stopped.

We'd played right into it, right into his apartment. Alone. Fear gripped my stomach as I thought about Alex, sitting out there with Dylan while I was in here. A little relief washed over me at the memory of his gun. The guy could take care of himself. But here I'd gone and separated us. Setting my jaw, I flushed the toilet, then splashed a little water on my face to cool it down before turning it off. I needed to get back out there.

I opened the bathroom and peered out. My heart settled as I heard Alex's voice. He had moved onto asking about Kevin, probably following the theory that Matt killed James, so Kevin beat up Matt. The relief was temporary, however, as I remembered him standing in the kitchen, near all of those knives.

Glancing at the calendar once more as I tiptoed passed the desk, my gaze landed on this week. Not only was there a crude circle marking today, but the words "The Cabin" were scrawled inside. But Dylan was here, not at a cabin. Unsure what that meant, I headed back out to be near Alex.

"Anything more you can give us about Grady?" Alex

asked as I returned. I'd almost forgotten Grady had been on our list of suspects, mostly because his motive hadn't seemed like enough.

"We heard some talk about the possible move affecting Grady's dad since he owned the house they were using for frat headquarters," Alex said.

Dylan waved a hand at us. "From what I could tell, the fight was really dumb. It was more Grady grasping at straws. His dad would probably actually come out ahead if they decided to move out of the cabin."

"The cabin?" I asked, voice croaking around the two words.

Alex's eyes narrowed almost imperceptibly as he read my probably manic body language. He focused back on Dylan, and I appreciated him not drawing attention to my weirdness. He must know I'd found something.

"Yeah, that's what they call the house they live in. Grady's dad's been giving them a huge discount on rent for years."

The frat house was called the cabin. Either Dylan was planning to pay them a visit or he already had. We needed to catch him before he could get out of here. Which meant I needed to prove his alibi was fake.

"So," I said, hoping my voice didn't sound as shaky as it felt. When he looked over at me, I continued. "You and your roommate get along pretty well?"

He nodded, but I could see a hint of worry behind his eyes.

"You said you two were hanging out, playing video games Friday night?" I held his gaze with so much more confidence than I felt.

Dylan's eyes flicked between me and Alex, his cheeks

growing slightly red. "I—uh—there's…" He let out a whoosh of breath. "No. I'm so sorry. I lied."

Blinking, I tried not to laugh in triumph. That was *way* easier than I thought it was going to be. I could feel Alex sit up straighter in the stool next to me. I wondered if his hand was making its way toward his holster.

"Oh? What were you really doing?" I asked after Dylan didn't elaborate.

He met my eyes. "I was with another girl. I didn't want Chloe to find out."

The kitchen lights seemed to amplify, growing all too bright and buzzing in their florescent tubes. *What?* I almost coughed. That wasn't a confession. Looking to Alex, I tried to get my thoughts to line up after the veritable bowling ball Dylan had just thrown into them.

"You're… cheating on her?" I asked, incredulous.

"Yeah. I mean, Chloe's great and all, but she's so intense sometimes and—well, I met this new girl. Gina, is her name. She doesn't know about Chloe, either, and I was trying to keep it that way." He swallowed and smiled, but it seemed more like a cringe. "Honestly, I thought I might even get away with it."

"Did you lie to the police as well?" Alex asked, I noticed not admitting he was also part of the force. yet.

Dylan nodded. "I'm sorry, I just knew they'd be talking with Chloe and I didn't want it to sound suspicious when our stories didn't match."

Questions came running at me like too many excited Hammys and I couldn't seem to grab onto a single one in my bombarded state.

"Wait…" I squeezed my eyes shut for a moment. That was it… I had been wrong about Dylan.

But then I remembered the handwriting, the calendar

hanging in his bedroom. No. He was the killer—he had to be. My pulse ratcheted up as Dylan placed his hand on the counter. His fingers were now mere inches away from the large knife.

While I knew Alex was most likely seeing the same thing and would have his gun ready if Dylan did come at us, I searched nearby for anything I might use to block his attack. There was a large accounting textbook sitting on the counter to my left. I carefully lifted my hand and curled my fingers around the edge of the binding. In the process, I moved one of the pieces of mail sitting on top. The small address window, which had been covered before, was now fully in view. And I sucked in a quick breath.

Liam Emsworth.

Emsworth? Like Ethan?

Dylan had simply introduced him as Liam at the coffee shop. Eyes closing for a quick second, I pictured him standing in front of Nate. He'd been much shorter than the tall barista, but would've been just a few inches shorter than James. Just like the detective had said.

I couldn't breathe. Glancing behind me, I looked through the open door to the second bedroom, the one I hadn't walked through to get to the bathroom. Dirty clothes littered every surface, and a few large baseball posters were pinned to the wall. Dylan had lost his baseball scholarship. I gulped. That was his room, which meant…

I'd walked through Liam's room to get to the bathroom.

It was Liam who'd written the journal, Liam who was at the campground that night, and Liam who was Ethan's brother.

"What do you want me to do?" Dylan asked. "I'll go to the police, tell them the truth." He moved the hand closest to the knife, but he didn't pick up the weapon, instead moving the hand through his hair.

I reached out under the counter and grabbed onto Alex's arm, hoping his presence might steady me.

"Dylan," I said, warily.

He looked up.

"How long have you and Liam lived together?" I asked.

He blinked. "Just a few months. Why?"

My mouth felt hot, tasted of iron, and the apartment felt like it was tipping.

"Why didn't you tell us he was the one who saved your life during the hazing, that he was the other pledge?"

Alex turned to face me. The color drained from Dylan's face.

"Liam wrote the journal, Alex. Not James."

20

As Alex sat there in shock, everything else clicked into place. The journal had been too full, too detailed to have been created in the few months since Dylan had attempted to rush for the TriAlphas. It looked like years of work, years of research.

Just about three years, I was betting.

I kept an eye on Dylan who still hadn't answered any of my questions. "Where was Liam when you were out with Gina on Friday night?"

Dylan swallowed. Shook his head. "I don't know. Here?"

"Was he here when you came back that night?" I asked, trying not to yell in my frustration.

At this, Dylan blinked. "He was here when I came back… in the morning. I stayed with Gina."

"So he could've been gone all night." Turning wild eyes on Alex, I said, "It was Liam. He killed James and tried to kill Matt. And now…" My stomach sank as I remembered the circle on the calendar in Liam's room. "Oh no. The cabin. Do you know where Liam is right now?"

Dylan shrugged. "I don't know, it's his brother's birthday

—or, would've been. He said he needed some time alone." He began pacing in the kitchen. "Wait, you really think he could've killed those guys?"

"You tell us. He's your roommate," Alex said flatly.

The color drained from Dylan's features.

I stood up, rushing toward the door. "Dylan, you need to show us where the TriAlphas house is."

Alex's hand was on his holster, but he didn't need to use it because Dylan nodded, and followed me without hesitation.

"I promise I didn't know about any of this. I hate the guys, but I don't want anyone to die." Dylan rambled on as we ran toward Alex's truck.

We stayed silent as we clambered inside and Alex peeled out, following the distraught Dylan's directions.

After a few minutes, Dylan pointed to a large, white house. "There. It's that one."

This part of Pine Crest was known for its big houses with elaborate gardens. The house Dylan pointed at was huge—three stories, at least, with white columns flanking the large front steps. And while the yard was grand, holding huge rhododendrons and lilacs among other things, it looked overgrown and poorly cared for.

Alex parked the truck along the road and then pulled out his phone. He dialed a number and it began to ring. "Dad, I know who killed James and attacked Matt. I think he's going to hurt more people. I'm sending you my location. Come as soon as you can, with backup." He hung up, pushed the screen a few more times, then clicked off his phone. "Stay here."

"Alex." His name was a plea on my lips. "Let me come with you."

Jaw tight, he shook his head.

"What should I do?" Dylan's eyes were wide.

"You make sure she stays." Alex pointed at me. "Other than that, just wait until I come back or the police arrive." At that, he pulled out his gun, cocked it, and left.

Stepping carefully along the house, he skirted around the back and out of my line of sight. My heart hammered in my chest. Everything felt too hot. The cab of the truck was closing in on me the longer Alex was in there.

"Oh man. I can't believe Liam would do this," Dylan whined as his body began to bunch up, looking as uncomfortable as I felt. "The guy saved my life, you know."

I nodded, remembering Gregory talking about the shots and the Thoreau questions. Turning to face Dylan, I asked, "How many questions did you miss?" If I was stuck here. I might as well take my mind off Alex alone inside that big house.

"Nine before I passed out."

"How many did Liam miss?"

Dylan gulped. "None. He knew them all."

Eyebrows raised, I turned back to the house. And my heart stopped. Walking up to the house was the redhead Kevin had been sweet-talking yesterday in the library, inviting her over tonight.

No, no, no… My eyes widened as she jogged up the front steps. I didn't know if Alex had made it inside yet, but I held my breath and hoped he was somewhere safe and hidden as she lifted her hand to knock at the front door.

I watched the redhead bang her fist three times on the glossy, black front door, sure I looked just like Hammy did whenever I made her wait for a treat—body quivering, eyes locked. After knocking, the redhead cocked her hip… then tapped her foot. Pulling out her phone, she checked it, then clicked it off and pivoted to face the other direction.

Releasing the breath I'd been holding, I let my body relax as she started down the steps.

But instead of walking back toward the street, the way she'd come, she started walking around the house, heading for the backyard.

"Wait. Where's she going?" My voice was frantic as I pressed my hand up against the truck window. Kevin's words from the library came to mind. *If we don't answer the door…* and then he'd whispered the rest. "Is there a back door?" I asked before realizing the stupidity of my question. Of course they had a back door.

"I only came here twice and I used the front door both times." Dylan said with a shrug, taking my stupid question seriously.

Whipping around to face him, I widened my eyes. "Stay here."

Dylan's mouth dropped open, but he didn't even have a chance to utter a syllable before I opened the door and jumped out of the truck. My feet flew across the springy green grass in my pursuit of the redhead. If Alex had gotten in through the back door and it was open, she could be walking into a whole lot of trouble.

My shoes crunched as I transitioned from the grass onto a stone pathway that led into a backyard equally as overgrown as the front. I stopped short once I could see the whole yard and sucked in a quick breath.

No one was there.

But… she had been just in front of me—ten seconds ahead at the most. There was no way she could've already scaled the back steps, opened the door, and shut it behind her. Deep creases formed in my forehead as I surveyed the rest of the yard.

Toward the middle of the space, a small, algae-infested

pond rippled with the occasional bug touching down on its surface. So their cabin had a pond, too. Though, I had to admit this one was not emitting the serene vibes I imagined Walden would. In fact, this water feature only added to the eerie, uncomfortable feeling rising up the back of my neck.

Or maybe that feeling had more to do with the redhead flat out disappearing back here seconds earlier.

Where had she gone? Was she hiding somewhere?

Walking forward, I searched for any movement, anything out of the ordinary, a flash of that red hair. There were tall, woody lilacs bordering the property, along with a tall fence. Leafy, green rhodies crowded untended walkways while weeds sprouted up in between.

Overgrown as the plants were, I still couldn't see any area she could've used to hide. The fence ran continuously along the three sides of the yard, so unless she went back around to the front of the house, she wasn't back here. I turned to face the house and that's when I noticed it.

Butting up right against the back corner of the porch was a small shed. A shed was definitely a hiding spot, but what caught my attention most was the white, striped snake, spray painted via stencil onto the bottom part of the shed door. The striped snake from *Walden*, Thoreau's symbol for the common man, numb and oblivious.

Glancing up at what looked to be one of the bedrooms, I noticed a shadow moving through the window. Alex must be upstairs. He was too far away to help the girl and she might not have time for me to get his attention. It was up to me.

Following the snake, I jogged over to the shed, opening the door as quietly as I could. Inside, it took my eyes a moment to adjust from the brilliant summer sunshine to the musty darkness, but once they did, the hairs on my arm tingled as they raised slightly. I wasn't sure if it was from the cold or out of fear, but it was probably a mixture of the two as I stared down a set of dark steps instead of the inside of a garden shed.

Feet fueled by necessity—I had to find that redhead before she became one more victim on the list Liam had begun—I ran down the steps, skidding to a stop at the bottom. But apparently I didn't stop quickly enough, because what I expected to be a solid door at the end of the staircase turned out to be a dark curtain of fabric and I fell forward into a well-lit room, stumbling on something at my feet.

Liam stood right in front of me, pointing a gun at me.

"Another one?" He shook his head, annoyance leaking from his pores.

That was when I glanced down, noticing for the first time what I'd stumbled over. It was the redhead, lying in a crumpled heap at my feet. I wanted to cry, to scream, to yell, but then I remembered that I hadn't heard a gun shot. The relief that surged through me at the realization that he must've just conked her over the head was short lived as I looked around.

I was in the basement. Kevin, Grady, and two more of the frat guys I recognized but couldn't name, sat tied to chairs in the middle of the basement. They were slumped over, eyes either blinking at me deliriously or completely closed.

"I know you," Liam said, watching me, still holding the gun level with my chest. He moved closer and I thought he was going to knock me unconscious, too, but he said, "It's my turn to ask some questions." Using his gun, he motioned to a chair in the corner. "Sit."

When I did, he wrapped a length of rope tightly around

my ankles and the legs of the chair. I stifled a yip as he cinched it tight and knotted it. Then checking around him on the floor, he seemed to come up empty-handed because he let out a low growl. "Looks like that's the last of my rope, but if you try anything, *anything*, I will not hesitate to shoot you."

Trying to breathe through the fear clawing at my throat, I nodded.

"You were the girl asking Dylan questions the other day."

I nodded.

"Where's your boyfriend?"

"At work." Not *technically* a lie.

"You came here alone?"

Another nod.

Liam narrowed his eyes, staring at me as if he were trying to stare into my body, to see my brain. Finally, he said, "Your boyfriend did say you have some weird Nancy Drew complex. I guess you seem dumb enough to run in here alone, thinking you can save everyone."

I gulped.

That seemed like enough of an answer for him, because he tucked the gun into the back waistband of his jeans then grabbed a large bottle of vodka and a funnel with a rubber tube attached. Walking over to Kevin, he positioned himself in front of the hunched shape. He tilted Kevin's head back so he could stick the tube in his mouth, then proceeded to pour the vodka into the funnel. Kevin, who I'd thought was completely passed out, sputtered and coughed, but Liam held his hand over his mouth.

"That's it. Drink. Drink yourselves to death. Just like you made Ethan do."

With a sick smile, he turned to Grady.

"You're killing them!" I cried, my body wanting to run over to help them. Sure my hands were untied and I could try to reach down and untie my feet, but my mind was bound by the fear of the gun Liam had tucked in the waistband of his pants.

"Uh… yeah," he said, turning toward me and rolling his eyes.

"They'll catch you. You'll never get away with *this*." I realized that I'd now become part of that ominous *this*. Would Liam kill me, too? In that moment, I restrained myself from looking up, listening for Alex. If Liam didn't know Alex was up there, we still had the upper hand.

"Under a government which imprisons unjustly, the true place for a just man is also a prison," Liam said, quoting *Civil Disobedience*.

He moved back toward Grady, who glanced over at me blearily before Liam shoved the tube in his mouth. From the wetness coating their shirts and the ground around them, I'd say Liam had been at this for a while. My stomach churned at the sight, and I searched around wildly for anything that might help.

"Who did Thoreau plant a garden for as a wedding present?" Liam asked the guy next to Grady.

He mumbled something and shook his head.

"Oh, sorry. The answer was Nathaniel Hawthorne and his wife Sofia. I guess you'll have to drink, just like my brother." Liam shoved the tube into the poor guy's mouth and began pouring again.

I felt like puking as the prisoner gagged and tried to fight his restraints. Even though I wasn't wholly tied up, I was just as imprisoned as these young men, knowing if I moved I would have that gun pointed at me again. I tried hard to think of anything I could do. I knew Alex's backup would be here any moment, but these guys might not have moments with the way Liam was dumping booze down their throats.

Closing my eyes, I thought back to something my father used to say whenever we went hiking. "All good things are wild and free."

My eyes flashed open. My body may not be free, but my mind was. And little did he know it, but my father had prepared me for this very moment.

"Liam," I said softly.

He glanced over at me, wild in his movements and expression.

Taking a deep breath, I tried to remember everything I could. "It is not a man's duty to devote himself to the eradication of any, even the most enormous wrong. And he must not pursue them sitting upon another man's shoulders." I knew I was paraphrasing, but I think I hit the main idea.

Liam stalked over to me, my words seeming to have only stoked the fire in his expression. "These are but improved means to an unimproved end," he shot back, sneering.

A creaking sounded from the top of the basement steps, from the door leading inside the house, not the secret entrance in the garden. Alex. He had found me. Liam turned his head, listening.

Inwardly cringing, I frantically tried to think of a way to distract Liam. With how well my last quote had caught his attention, I thought back to any more Thoreau I could remember.

My father's words floated through my mind. I was ten. It had been a bad day, I was curled up on my bed telling my father I wished I could be Tracy Stevens because she had beautiful, blond hair and their family went to France every summer. And he'd told me…

"Fools stand on their island of opportunities and look toward another land. There is no other land; there is no other life but this, Liam." I almost smiled, happy at my ability to remember, but then I noticed the anger smoldering in his features and I gulped it back. "I know you're mad about your brother, and you're right; what happened was not okay. But it doesn't mean you have to become just like them. We can reopen the case, find justice for your brother's death."

Liam tilted his head as he listened. I must've been channeling my father in that moment, between the calm, cooing quality of my voice and the quotes. The memory of him wrapped around me like a bulletproof vest. I was getting through to Liam, I could see his shoulders dropping, his attention flitting back to the frat guys in the chairs, away from the basement stairs.

But his shoulders stiffened; he stood up straight, and his eyes glazed over with a terrifying anger. "There are a thousand hacking at the branches of evil, but I am striking at the root." He moved to spin away.

Which was when I saw my opportunity.

My skin pricked with anticipation as I lunged at his back, bringing the chair my feet were tied to with me. I grabbed at the gun he'd left tucked into his waistband. He spun around throwing his bodyweight into me as I fumbled the pistol. It clattered to the floor, skidding off underneath the staircase.

Liam's gaze met mine. I jumped onto him as he scrambled forward toward the gun. The chair clanged away behind me as I finally kicked free of the rope that bound my ankles. My mouth went dry. For a second everything felt like that recurring nightmare where I desperately needed to yell but I didn't have a voice.

Swallowing, I tried again. This time, it worked. "Alex! Now!"

Tears crowded my eyes as I heard the door bang open and footsteps thundered down the basement stairs. Alex was first down, but a group of Pine Crest's finest followed closely behind. Alex reached me, pulling me up into his arms once he was sure the other officers had Liam under control. Liam's hand was only inches away from the gun when they grabbed it and cuffed it behind his back.

The basement was a confusing cacophony of noise and movement. I could hear Detective Valdez's voice through the din, calling for ambulances as he knelt to help the frat guys. Liam yelled, kicking out and throwing his body as the officers took him away, leading him up the stairs.

Alex squeezed me close, kissing the top of my head. "Are you okay?"

I looked up at him, nodding. "I'm sorry. I know you told me to stay in the truck, but she came into the picture and…" I motioned to the redhead who was slowly coming to with the help of one of the officers. "I tried to stop her, but I failed."

"I wouldn't say that," Detective Valdez said from a few feet away where he knelt next to Grady.

Alex and I turned to look at him. Three other officers had taken over untying Kevin and the others, so the detective stood and walked toward us.

Before he could say anything more, our attention turned to the stairs, where EMTs were now streaming down. After a quick check for vitals, the first responders took the fraternity members and the redhead upstairs to load them into the aid cars and to the hospital.

In the relative silence which followed, the detective added, "They owe their lives to you. If you hadn't figured out who the killer was, we never would've made it in time." He dipped his chin at me and gave me a warm smile. "You know, you wouldn't make a bad officer, Pepper."

Thinking of my dad, I shook my head. "I think I'll stick with the literature. It's in my blood."

21

Two weeks later…

A LATE SUMMER breeze brushed its fingers through my hair. I closed my eyes and leaned my head out the open truck window.

"Learning to Fly" by Tom Petty crooned from Alex's speakers and transported me back in time.

For a moment, I was with my dad, walking through the forest, listening to Petty and quoting Thoreau. Then I drifted back into reality, into the cab of Alex's truck, driving through the streets of Pine Crest. My chest ached with how much I still missed my dad, but these days it almost felt like he was walking right next to me, like he'd never left.

Hamburger pounced onto my lap, sticking her face out the window and snorting happily in the last bit of wind as Alex pulled the truck into my mom's driveway—sorry, Mom and Duncan's driveway. They were finally moved in together and were having us over for a housewarming party.

Congratulating Duncan on taking my father's place in our old house felt like the most confusing thing ever.

Alex parked next to Maggie and Josh's car, turned off the engine, and smiled at me.

"Ready?"

I nodded. Scooping Hammy into my arms, I got out of the car and started down the driveway. Alex plucked the hanging basket we got them out of the truck bed and followed behind.

"I want Mom to be happy. I like Duncan. He's nice. I don't mind him living in my childhood home at all," I mumbled to myself as I walked up the path. Hammy must've thought I was speaking to her, because she looked up and licked my cheek.

Alex's hand landed on the small of my back just as we stepped up to the front door. I took a deep breath and then knocked.

Mom swung open the front door, a huge grin on her face. "Welcome! Come in."

We walked forward and Alex held out the basket. "Happy housewarming."

"That's so sweet of you two. Everyone's in the kitchen if you want to head in." Mom pointed to the kitchen as if I might've forgotten where it was, as if I hadn't grown up here. "I'm going to go hang these beauties on the porch." She took the flowers and scurried off toward the back of the house.

I heard my sister's loud laugh float out from the kitchen, so I unclipped Hammy from her leash and set her down to roam free. The moment her feet hit the hardwoods, she flattened her ears and scurried into the kitchen as if the large gray cat from our neighborhood were chasing after her.

"Hammy!" my niece, Brooklyn, exclaimed at the same

moment I heard Ham's claws scrape and slide onto the tile of the kitchen floor. Hudson, the toddler, squealed with delight.

Alex and I followed in the wake of the little dog, knowing full well she was the main event as far as the kids were concerned. When we walked into the kitchen, Josh was playing with the kids and now Hammy in the adjoining family room, and Duncan and Maggie were chatting over by plates of hors d'oeuvres set out on the island. Maggie let out another long laugh, swiping happy tears from her eyes.

I almost got mad at her for being so friendly with the new guy in our mother's life, but then I remembered I wanted my mom to be happy. I liked Duncan, and I didn't care he was moving into my childhood home.

"Oh, Peps." Maggie's eyes lit up as she noticed me. "Duncan was just telling me some of the craziest stories about the favors his actors used to ask him."

Up until last summer, Duncan had been a manager to some pretty big-name stars in Hollywood.

I smiled and said, "Fun!" instead of jabbing her with an elbow and reminding her we were supposed to be mad at him together.

"I have to say," Maggie sighed and glanced around. "I had a little bit of trouble with it at first, but…" Maggie nodded approvingly. "Your stuff looks really good in here."

Wrinkling my nose, I popped some undefined puff pastry into my mouth and pretended to be too invested in chewing to add my two cents. At twenty-eight, Maggie was five years older than me, so I supposed it made sense for her to have a more mature take on the situation. But still, I hated being alone in my discomfort.

Duncan beamed at Maggie and then me, but then my mother entered the room and the man practically glowed.

He wrapped an arm around Mom's waist, handed her a glass, and then raised his own.

"Well, now we're all here, I'd love to make a toast."

Alex showed up next to me, handing over a glass of sparkling wine.

"While I would love to thank you, Lilly, and your beautiful family for accepting me so generously into their lives, I would be completely remiss to leave out the most important person in this equation. So this evening, I propose the most hearty of toasts to the unforgettable Jackson Brooks."

Hearing Duncan say my father's name felt like a slap to the face. And from the way the rest of the people in the room were blinking and gripping their drinks tight, I would say I wasn't the only one. As if he could read my thoughts and knew I needed a little more support, Alex slid his arm around my shoulders, pulling me tight to him.

"I've seen a lot of families in my day, a lot of heartache, too." Duncan stopped and smiled sadly at my mother.

And it hit me. Other than the nature of his previous job, I knew very little about Duncan's life. I had no idea what he'd gone through before meeting my mother.

Taking a deep breath, Duncan continued. "But never have I encountered a family hold so fiercely to the memory of one man while, at the same time, moving on with their lives so gracefully. He must've been a special man to illicit such a perfect legacy."

A hot tear dripped onto my arm and I realized I was crying.

Duncan raised his glass higher. "So this is for you, Jackson. This family of yours needs no looking after in your wake. But I sure am glad they decided to look after me."

We all raised our glasses, clinking them together while saying either, "To Dad" or "To Jackson." Tears glinted in the corners of Mom's eyes and I noticed Maggie had a few tears running down her face just like me. Once I'd touched everyone else's glass with my own, I took a long sip, letting the bubbles fizz and run down my throat.

In that moment, I was reminded once again of Thoreau's saying, "Things do not change; we change." And I could… would. Just because I'd had a hard time accepting Duncan into my family at first didn't mean it always had to be that way, and just because Dad was gone didn't mean we were doing anything wrong by letting someone else into our lives.

Glancing over at the family room where the kids were still playing, unaware of the sniffly-emotion-fest happening in the kitchen, my attention fell on a beautiful, carved-wood end table.

"Maggie's right, Duncan. You have some beautiful pieces. They really do look good in here." I motioned to the table.

Duncan said thank you, but was quickly interrupted by Josh who sighed and said, "Okay, but now can we finally talk about the most important thing in the room?"

We all blinked, everyone seeming just as unsure as I was about what Josh was referring to.

"The elephant?" Josh looked to me. "Pepper being held at gunpoint by someone in the very fraternity which your dad helped create thirty years ago." He glanced around the kitchen. "Am I the only one who finds this crazy?"

"Technically, the killer wasn't part of the fraternity," I said, holding up a finger to correct Josh. But then I exhaled loudly. "You're right that it was crazy, though. I have to say, I thought I was stressed out with grad classes and the bookstore, but I think my mini vacation from both made me miss my normal life, as hectic as it can be at times. I'm just glad everything worked out relatively well in the end."

Not only had the paramedics been able to get the fraternity members to the hospital in time to save them from the copious amounts of hard alcohol Liam had dumped down their throats, but Matt had finally woken up and was headed out of intensive care. He'd been able to identify Liam as his attacker, not that the police needed him to; they'd found one of Liam's prints on the knife Sheriff Langley had finally turned in, after a little pressing from a fellow TriAlpha. I sent a silent thank you to Mr. Wilford.

"Did you see Gregory Wilford put out a press release about the fraternity, calling all alumni to cease and desist any special treatment for other members or they would be answering to the police?" Mom asked, of course latching onto the legal aspect of the case.

I nodded, smiling at the article he'd gotten Chloe to write up for him. "Yeah, I can't believe he's stepping down as dean of students, but I'm happy he made an example of Sheriff Langley by calling him out on his obstruction of justice."

"I'm just grateful he didn't include Dad's name in any of it. That was a pretty big deal for him to take credit for the whole idea," Maggie said.

"I don't think your father or Gregory could've ever foreseen it growing into what it did," Mom added.

"It's not what you look at that matters, it's what you see," I said with a shrug. Everyone turned to me. "Dad looked at Thoreau's work and saw empowerment, a call to action, a chance to better our lives and others'. Liam saw an excuse to eschew the law and take a situation into his own hands." I looked down at my glass. "I'm just sorry I ever questioned

Dad, that I ever thought he could have any part in the darkness which overcame the fraternity."

Mom placed a supportive hand on my shoulder and gave it a squeeze. I glanced over at Alex, expecting him to chastise me for yet another Thoreau quote.

Instead, he said, "It's not until we are lost that we begin to find ourselves."

A big smile spread across my face. "I thought you hated Thoreau."

He shrugged. "He's growing on me. Plus, I paraphrased that quote."

"Oh, I know," I said with a wink. "But I love you for it anyway."

———

DON'T MISS PEPPER'S NEXT ADVENTURE:

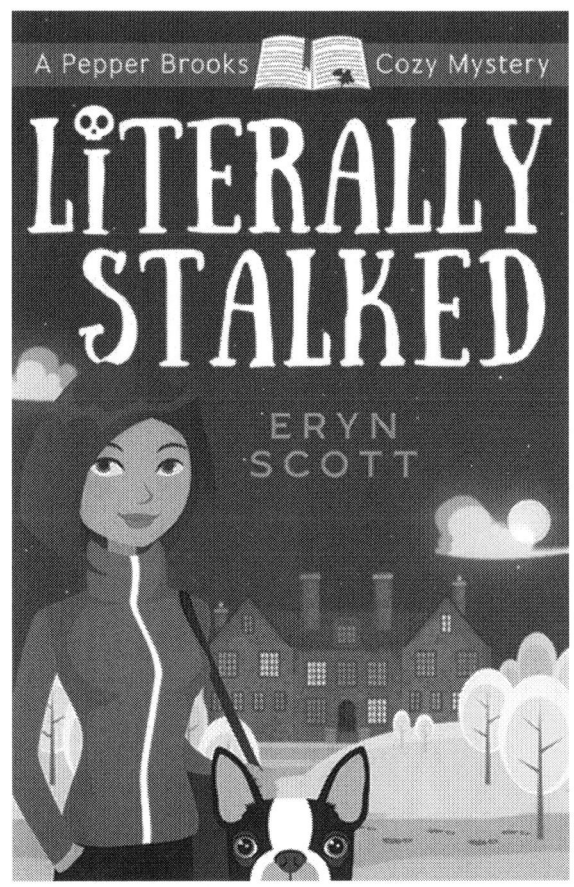

A Pepper Brooks Cozy Mystery

LITERALLY STALKED

ERYN SCOTT

"I love you to death"

Winter quarter of grad school has Pepper living and breathing Brontë sisters. When a body is found near the mysterious mansion on the hill, Pepper is too close to the victim for comfort… and perhaps the killer.

Pepper's interest in the case becomes an obsession when Alex is threatened. Between mysterious notes, long-buried secrets, and that feeling someone is watching, Pine Crest starts to feel a whole lot like the gothic moors of Wuthering Heights. The line between love and obsession is as thin as a knife's blade—literally—and it's up to Pepper to find the killer before they strike again.

Get your copy!

ALSO BY ERYN SCOTT

Mystery:

The Pepper Brooks Cozy Mystery Series

The Stoneybrook Mysteries

Women's fiction:

The Beauty of Perhaps

Settling Up

The What's in a Name Series

In Her Way

Romantic comedy:

Meet Me in the Middle

ABOUT THE AUTHOR

Eryn Scott lives in the Pacific Northwest with her husband and their quirky animals. She loves classic literature, musicals, knitting, and hiking. She writes women's fiction and cozy mysteries.

Join her mailing list to learn about new releases and sales!

www.erynwrites.com
erynwrites@gmail.com

Printed in Great Britain
by Amazon